THE CAREY GUN

Thomas Carey Westerns
Book Three

Irving A Greenfield

THE CAREY GUN

Published by Sapere Books.

24 Trafalgar Road, Ilkley, LS29 8HH

saperebooks.com

ISBN: 978-1-80055-771-0

ONE

Major Thomas Carey hunkered close to the low fire. Other Confederate soldiers like himself, hoping to drive the numbness from their fingers and coax some warmth into the rest of their chilled bodies, extended their bare hands toward the unsteady flames.

Thomas, a tall, lean, gaunt-faced man from southwest Texas, flexed his fingers several times, took a few moments to roll and light a cigarette, and then stood up to make way for another man.

He inhaled deeply, savoring the sharp bite of the cigarette smoke. All around him, but protected from the deadly accuracy of the Union sharpshooters by an earthen breastworks, were dozens of small red winking fires, each with its particular circle of unshaven, haggard-looking men, all of whom were strangers to him. They were infantry, though there were some artillerymen among them. But so far as Thomas knew, he was the only cavalryman there.

Assigned to act as liaison officer in the initial stages of the attack, Thomas would lead two troops of cavalry against Grant's communications once the Confederate infantry had breached the federal line with the capture of Fort Stedman and the three fortifications behind it.

Thomas did not like the assignment. He did not understand what General Lee hoped to gain by attacking Grant. So far as he was concerned, Grant had already beaten Lee fair and square, and it would just be a matter of time before Lee would own up to it. And the idea of not having a horse under him for even part of the action made Thomas feel uneasy, as though he had forgotten something and could not remember what it was.

He took another deep drag on the cigarette. The smoke rushed out of his nostrils and instantly vanished into the blackness of the night. Taking what was left of the cigarette out of his mouth. Thomas snuffed out the burning end with his fingers and put the butt in his coat pocket.

He was about to find a place where he could stretch out for a while when he saw General Gordon talking to the three guides who would lead the attacking force to the three Union forts behind Stedman.

The general was a tall man with a full black beard, a strong nose, and sharp black eyes. It was hard to tell if he was naturally thin or, like all of the other men in the Confederate Army, suffering from hunger.

Thomas had heard the general's name a few times before he had reported to the man for the briefing in the command tent, which was several hundred yards to the rear of the breastworks. He was said to be a middling good commander, but very covetous of his reputation.

The general had made short work of what he had to say. He had impressed Thomas as a 'no-nonsense' man.

'The plan,' Gordon had told them in his slow Georgia drawl, 'is simple. Our men will take Fort Stedman and the adjacent Battery Ten, they will advance to the three positions beyond Stedman, and then they will turn the Yankee guns on Grant's rear. This will enable our cavalry to go through and get behind the federal lines. It will also make Grant shorten his lines.' He went on to detail how he expected to achieve such a stunning blow with only three columns of one hundred men.

Thomas listened very carefully to everything that Gordon said. Even in the yellow light of the command tent, the general's black eyes glowed with a certainty that probably inspired the other officers with confidence but made Thomas wary of him, especially when he called upon the Almighty to acknowledge the righteousness of the cause for which they were fighting by granting them victory.

Thomas had fought long enough, had killed enough, and had lived enough during his twenty-five years to know that God, if He existed, did not win victories. Men won them, and the winning had — as far as Thomas could see — absolutely nothing to do with the cause.

The general ended the briefing by telling his officers, 'Of course, we will be supported by other army units. General Lee doesn't expect us to lick the whole Yankee army all on our own. But with the kind of men we've got, I don't doubt that we could do it.'

Polite laughter followed the general's words, and even Thomas smiled.

There was still pride and spirit in the tattered remnants of the Army of Northern Virginia as its thin lines of gaunt, hungry men stood between Grant and Petersburg, Virginia. It could still fight.

If the officers and men of the army possessed nothing else, they had through the ordeal of four years of war gained a deep respect for each other, a comradeship that could come only when each had been put to the supreme test and had survived.

In the past Thomas had not thought too much about the men he had come to know in the army, but now that the end of the war seemed close at hand, he wondered how many of them had, like himself, killed, suffered, and endured because it still was — for all its danger better than what they had at home. His reason for joining up had nothing to do with his feeling for the South's cause. He did not believe that any man should own another, and neither did he think that any state should be as strong as the Federal Government. He had joined the army back in '61 to get away from his father and to escape from his marriage to Helen.

None of Thomas' thinking was in the least bit organized. It came in bits and pieces. Mostly it was disconnected, but such as it was, it gave him a reason to look back on all the things that had happened to him. How he discovered that his father had hired a man to kill him. How even as he killed his would-be murderer he was captured by the Yankees. How he escaped and made his way back to the old ranch in Paso Diablo to kill his father, only to find that the old man had died some months before. And how he looked down at his father's grave and realized how much he really loved him. And how he came, if not to love Helen, then to respect her. And, finally, how he left the ranch for a second time to go back to war because there was nowhere else for him to go, and nothing more for him to do, until the war was done with.

Even if the attack on Fort Stedman would make Grant shorten his lines, Thomas knew that the Army of the Confederacy was at bay. It was like the last desperate rush of a dying wolf. Grant would kill it soon, but Thomas was determined to stay with it until the end. That much he owed to the men who had died fighting beside him. It was a debt he had to pay. Perhaps that was the real reason he had returned to the army the second time.

'Are there any questions?' the general asked after a short pause. There were none, and after reminding his staff that the attack would begin at four in the morning, he dismissed them.

Thomas watched the general and the three guides until they moved out of the overlapping reddish-colored penumbras from several nearby fires and disappeared into the deep shadows.

Had the general lingered for a few more moments, Thomas would have asked him how he could be so certain that the attack would take the Yankees by surprise. But, realizing he had missed the opportunity, he shrugged and headed for a place on the slope of the breast works, where he sat down and waited for the attack to begin.

According to the general's plan, men had already removed obstructions in front of Colquitt's Salient the previous night to give the attacking troops a sally port. All that effort had not aroused the Union lines, which began only a hundred and fifty yards away, or their pickets, which lay a scant fifty yards in front of the Confederate line.

Thomas put his hand in his pocket. He felt the half-finished cigarette, but decided to forego the pleasure of smoking it a while longer. He leaned back on the slope, and placing his hands behind his head, he looked up at the cloud-filled sky.

When he looked directly above him, and when he lowered his eyes to look beyond the red glow of the many campfires, there was nothing much for him to see except perhaps the darker shapes of several shell-blasted trees. Moving his line of vision to the more immediate vicinity, Thomas found himself wondering how many of the men he saw would be alive by midday.

Would *he* be alive?

It was a question he always asked himself before a battle, and never could he give an answer with any degree of certainty, or truthfulness. There was no way a man could know that he would be killed, though Thomas remembered having heard about many who had some sign of their own death in a dream or just a feeling.

He chuckled. His feelings, for whatever they were worth, always had him alive. And in his dreams he was the one who did the killing. If he was not killing, he was lying naked in bed with a woman.

The dreams of killing gave Thomas no pleasure except the sureness of his own life. But the dreams about a woman made him realize how long it had been since he had been with one. Even thinking about having a woman brought forth a warm feeling in his groin.

He shook his head, sat up, and, rubbing the stubble on his chin, decided that he would be better off not thinking about women until after the attack.

If I come out all right, he silently promised himself, *I'll make it a point to find a woman and celebrate.*

He caught the scent of freshly made coffee and decided to get some. Without hesitation he left the slope of the breastworks. Suddenly he remembered it was Saturday, March 25th, 1865. If he was lucky, he would be around to see Sunday.

Thomas stood some distance from one of the fires, but still close enough for the meager reddish glow to flutter across his face. He sipped at the steaming coffee. It tasted bitter, probably because it was heavily laced with chicory. But it was hot, and that made it tolerable.

He drank slowly from his tin cup until some of the sludge got into his mouth. He spat it out and swore under his breath. He took a few moments to wash his mouth out with water from his canteen and then moved back toward the fire.

'This time,' Thomas said, stooping down toward the man holding the coffee pot, 'try to give me more coffee and less grounds.'

The man looked up at him, shrugged, and answered, 'I don't have no say on how it comes out, sir.'

The other men around the fire shifted uneasily.

Thomas did not answer. He realized he had made a mistake by saying anything. The men were understandably edgy. When his cup was half filled he nodded, and once more withdrew from the circle of men around the fire.

''Scuse me, major,' one of the men called. Thomas stopped and turned. The man continued, 'Yer name be Carey? Thomas Carey?'

Thomas said nothing. He shifted his tin cup from his right to his left hand.

'You shor' look like him,' the man said. 'I mean, you're a dead ringer fer him … but he was a cap'in when I knowed him.'

'And when was that?' Thomas questioned in a tight but soft voice. The man who was standing less than a dozen paces in front of him did not look the least bit familiar. He was of middling height, light-haired, and because he was gaunt like the rest of the men, it was hard to judge his age.

'Sometime back,' the man answered, moving closer.

Thomas' right hand eased over his side arm.

The man's eyes followed the movement, and he stopped in his tracks.

'Where?' Thomas asked, still keeping his voice tight and soft.

'In a Yankee prison,' the man said. 'The Thomas Carey I knowed wuz a prisoner jest like me an' the rest o' the men. He wuz a cap'in —'

'So you told me.'

The man nodded and said, 'But I ain't told you about the Thomas Carey I knowed.'

Thomas glanced toward the breastwork.

'Maybe I could tell you better,' the man suggested, 'if'n we moved off a bit.'

'Back there,' Thomas answered, gesturing with his head toward the breastwork.

'I'll be right behind you.'

'Suppose you walk in front of me,' Thomas told him.

The man chuckled and began to walk. Thomas moved aside to let him pass and then followed, keeping several paces behind. Neither one spoke until they reached the slope. Then the man asked, 'Is it all right if'n I turn 'round now?'

'It's all right,' Thomas answered.

Thomas was closer to the man than he had been when they were near the fire. He could see that the man was about his age, give or take a year or two.

'What's your name?' Thomas asked.

'You wouldn't know me by name … I wuz jest one of the men who went wid you.' The man was obviously sure who he was. 'But maybe you recollect the name Jason?' he asked, grinning.

Thomas lifted his cup and took a sip of coffee. 'Suppose you tell me more?' he answered.

'An' there wuz Coomy,' the man said, 'who the Yankees kilt before we started that march to the railhead. We wuz all goin' to Rock Island Prison but you wuz goin' to lead us —' He stopped, and with a knowing chuckle he explained, 'But you kinda got lost in the snowstorm. You took the Yankee lootenant wid you an' you took his horse. Now a lot of the men on that march called you a no-good skunk for leavin' them that way … some even called you a lot worse. An' lots never made it to the railhead.'

'What happened?' Thomas questioned.

'Mind if'n I sit? Seems like I'll be usin' my feet a heap once the fightin' begins.'

'Sit,' Thomas answered, throwing the rest of the coffee out of his cup. It tasted even more bitter than the first cup, or maybe what the man was telling him made it seem so.

'You got a smoke?' the man asked.

Thomas dug into his coat pocket and pulled out the butt he had been saving.

'Thank you kindly,' the man said, reaching for it. He took time to find a match and light the cigarette. 'Nothin' like a smoke to put a man at his ease, except maybe a jug of good corn whisky and a full-titted woman, wouldn't you say, Major Carey?'

'What happened to the men —'

'I knowed,' the man told him, 'if'n I ever met up wid you, you'd be real interested in what happened after you run away.'

Thomas stiffened.

'That's what some of the men said,' the man was quick to explain, smiling up at Thomas. 'But I didn't hol' wid that. A man has a right to save his self when it comes down to it, now don't he?'

Thomas said nothing.

'See,' the man continued, 'after you whipped Jason good an' proper, the men kind of figured you'd save all of 'em. I mean, you wuz the only officer there, so we figured you'd act kind of proper. Nobody expected you to bug out like you did an' leave the rest of us.'

To ease the tightness in his throat, Thomas swallowed several times, but it would not go away.

'Some of the men said they knowed you wuz a polecat when Jason tol' 'em how you kilt that Zeb feller an' how you made up the story that your pa sent 'im to kill you. Now what pa'd do somethin' like that to his own son?'

'How many made it?' Thomas asked, ignoring the other man's question.

'Depends,' the man answered. 'If you mean to the railhead, I don't know. Most didn't … all those widout shoes didn't go no more than a few miles after we found you wuz gone. Would you believe it wuz ol' Jason who led us in the end? He turned out to be a right good soldier.'

'How many made it with him?'

'Countin' myself,' the man answered, 'there wuz ten of us.'

'Just ten?' Thomas questioned in a breathy voice.

'Would have been more, but some died on the way to the place where Coomy's friends had the horses. An' later some were kilt when we run into some Union cavalry. Ten of us made it back.'

'And the others?'

'Them that didn't die on the march might be alive … but I hear tell Rock Island is a hard place to keep alive in, isn't that so, Major Carey?'

Thomas nodded.

The man stood up, took a long drag on the cigarette, and then, dropping what was left to the ground, he crushed it under his heel. For several moments he kept his eyes cast downward. But then he looked straight at Thomas and said, 'I'm real glad to see that you're alive. Yes, sir. I'm glad it wuz me who saw you…' His thin lips curled back in a big smile. 'I'm goin' to kill you, majer,' he said. 'An if'n I don't do it, there'll be nine others who will. Yes, sir, majer, I'm right glad I met you!' he exclaimed. He turned and walked away.

Thomas drew, wheeled around, and found himself looking at the man's back. He wanted to shout a challenge, but instead he clenched his teeth so hard that pain stabbed at the sides of his jaw.

Slowly he put his gun up. A shudder passed through his body. And as he took several deep breaths to steady himself, he watched the man who had just spoken to him join the circle around the fire. There was no way for him to explain to that man — or, for that matter, to anyone else — that he could not have done anything other than what he had. The hate that had burned in Thomas for his father had kept him alive. How could another man understand that unless he had experienced it?

Thomas shook his head again. He could not even explain it to Jenny, the black woman who had given him shelter and food after he had escaped from the column of prisoners. Even after they had become lovers, he could not speak to her about it, and in the end he had left her, to do what he had started out to do…

Thomas shrugged. Had he been one of the ten who had successfully made it back to the Confederate lines, he too would have sworn an oath to kill the man who had deserted them. But more than one man had tried to kill him, and had failed.

Thomas looked at the man and then glanced at the breastworks. He had two enemies: the Yankees out there in the darkness, and the man behind him. He was sorry now that he had given away his last smoke.

TWO

Huddled in his threadbare gray coat, Thomas sat with his back against the wheel of a supply wagon. His head, cradled in his arms, rested on his drawn-up knees.

It seemed to have gotten colder. His old wounds ached, especially the one in his right shoulder. He had gotten it in a fight with Jason while they were both prisoners. Whenever the weather turned cold and damp it hurt, more than any wound made by a Yankee bullet or saber cut.

Thomas lifted his head, rubbed his right shoulder, and looked around. The fires were still burning, and a mist was beginning to snake up from Appomattox River, which was less than a mile to the southeast. If that mist continued to rise, it might go as high as Hare's Hill, where Fort Stedman was located, and —

He did not want to think of what could happen if the mist obscured their objectives. The mission was going to be difficult enough to accomplish without adding the problem of poor visibility to it.

Thomas stretched, and was about to resume his former position when he saw a man come toward him. He tensed and watched.

'You goin' out tonight, majer?' the man asked, standing over him.

'Yes,' Thomas answered, letting the looseness return to his rangy body.

'Then you best be wearin' one of these,' the soldier said, handing Thomas a crude white arm band. 'That's so all our boys will know each other.' He looked toward the rising mist and said, 'Seems like you'll be needin' them.'

Thomas stood up, muttered a thanks, and tied the white band around his arm.

'Good luck,' the soldier said.

'We'll need lots of it,' Thomas answered.

The man chuckled and walked away.

Thomas stretched again and checked his side arm, a five-shot .44 double-action revolver. He wore it low on his right side, with the holster secured to his right thigh with a thin strip of rawhide. It was not regulation, at least not the way he had it rigged. But neither was the coming battle a dress parade.

On his left side he carried a well-honed Bowie knife, which he had become adept at using. Later, when his mount was brought up, he would have an Enfield carbine and his saber.

Satisfied that his weapons were in working order, Thomas slowly walked around to the various fires, looking for the man who had been in prison with him. Though he was no longer particularly upset by the threat the man had made, he thought it would be a good idea for him to know where his would-be killer was, especially when the fight started and they would go up the open ground toward Fort Stedman. If the man would try to kill him, that would be a good time to do it...

The man was not at any of the fires, and Thomas could look for him among those men who were sleeping in various places around the encampment. But he had no doubt that they would find each other when the time came.

As the hour for the attack drew closer, the men behind the breastwork began to stir, awakened by some inner clock that drove sleep from their eyes and filled their bodies with a blood-pounding tension. Those who could not sleep checked and rechecked their weapons and ammunition, or let their eyes move restlessly to the sally port, out of which they would all too soon run to face another ordeal of fire and of possible death.

One by one the assault groups formed.

Thomas left on his own to join the fifty axmen, who would lead the attack, and whose mission it was to chop through the abatis and other obstacles in front of Fort Stedman. Had his life not been threatened, Thomas might have gone with one of the three assault groups, since he had no desire to be like the Biblical Uriah, in the forefront of the battle. But there were fewer axmen, and the man who had sworn to kill him was not among them.

Thomas presented himself to the young officer in charge of the detail and asked to accompany him.

'You may come with us,' the lieutenant said. 'But I must warn you that if you are wounded —'

'I understand,' Thomas told him.

The officer nodded and said, 'We go out at four.'

They saluted each other, and, concealing a smile, Thomas moved off to one side. The lieutenant was obviously inexperienced, and still believed that military courtesy should be observed even on the battlefield.

The minutes passed slowly. The men became restless. Thomas felt his stomach ball up into a knot…

Soon there were whispers that General Gordon was coming down to the breastwork to lead off the attack. Whether the general was there or not made little difference to Thomas, though he knew that some of the men might feel better for having seen him.

'Ready, men,' someone called. The cry was repeated over and over again.

The lieutenant in command of the axmen called them to readiness. A man near Thomas began to mumble a prayer. Then he looked at Thomas and said, 'If I ever get home to Lucy, I ain't never goin' to drink or fuck with another woman again, so help me God.' The man turned away and continued to pray.

Just as Thomas slipped his revolver free of the holster, General Gordon and several aides came down the breastworks. He stopped and spoke to every one of the officers who were in command of the assault groups. Then he came over to the lieutenant in charge of the axmen. After they had spoken for a few moments, the lieutenant ordered his men to the sally port. Thomas mixed with them and moved forward. The three guides were already waiting for the rifle shot that would signal the beginning of the attack on Fort Stedman.

The general mounted the breastwork and peered into the blackness beyond. A rifleman was with him. The man standing next to Thomas was breathing hard, and he himself felt a tightness in his chest.

Suddenly from the other side of the breastwork came the crash of timbers.

'What are you doing over there, Johnny?' a Yank challenged. 'What's that noise? Answer quick, or I'll shoot.'

'Never mind, Yank!' a Confederate soldier called back. 'Lie down an' go to sleep. We're jest a'gathin' a little corn ... you know, rations are mighty short over here.'

Laughter filtered through the darkness, and another voice said, 'Now if you rebs came over here you'd eat right good, or if you went on home, we'd all eat better'n what we're doin'.'

'You know ol' Marse Robert wouldn't like that a-tall,' the Confederate answered with a laugh. 'He's mighty particular about sech things.'

'Then I guess we'll have to whop you, like we've been doin', isn't that right, Johnny?'

'Can't say that it's to my liking,' the Southern soldier answered, keeping up a stream of chatter while the timbers were moved to provide a wider access path.

After a few minutes the men who were working beyond the breastwork returned through the sally port. General Gordon ordered the soldier with him to fire his rifle. The man lifted his weapon. The axmen tensed for the dash into the night. But the soldier did not fire.

'Shoot!' the general ordered.

The man still hesitated.

'Fire your gun, sir!' Gordon fumed.

'Why in God's name doesn't he fire?' the lieutenant questioned.

'He will,' Thomas answered, loud enough for the young officer to hear, 'as soon as he warns —'

'Hello, Yank,' a soldier shouted into the night. 'Wake up; we're a-goin' to shell the woods … look out; we're a-comin'!' Then he pulled the trigger. The shot split the stillness of the night with a single report.

The attack began.

The axmen rushed out after the guides. Other men followed. All of them ran up the mist-shrouded slope toward the top of Hare's Hill. They moved so fast that all the Yankee pickets were quickly killed or captured without their having to waste additional shots.

Breathless, Thomas ran up the hill. The mist was getting thicker. It would not be easy to bring two troops of horse soldiers into position…

Here and there, sometimes in front of him or running at his side, Thomas caught sight of some of the axmen. They were more like ghosts than men.

'Keep going, men,' the thin, almost quavering voice of the lieutenant urged. 'Keep going!'

Thomas gulped air. His heart was pounding, and his legs seemed to have turned to leaden weights. But he kept running with the rest of them. Sweat covered his body and dripped into his eyes.

'We're almost there!' the quavering voice sang out.

There was no way of telling how far they were from their goal. The mist shrouded everything.

'Halt!' A premonitory challenge rang out from somewhere deep in the mist. 'Who goes there?'

There was no time for anyone to answer. None of the men rushing up the hill dared to break stride and call out. And none had the breath to spare.

A shot rang out.

No one screamed. No one was hit.

Another shot slammed out from the depths of the thick swirling grayness.

'Oh my God!' a man shouted. 'Oh my God! I'm bleedin'. I'm bleedin'…

The man's cries dropped behind Thomas as he continued to run up the hill.

The sound of voices came drifting out of the mist. 'I tell ya, Mike,' the first said, 'that be Johnnies comin' up the hill.'

'How da hell did they get through our pickets?'

'Don't know, Al,' the other answered. 'But I sure as hell 'it one … you heard 'im bawlin' out there.'

Suddenly Thomas realized that one of the voices was in front of him. The figure took shape, grew darker.

'I see one,' the Yankee shouted. 'I see one!' He started to throw his rifle to his shoulder.

Thomas fired.

'Mike!' the man yelled. 'Mike, I'm gut-shot!'

Thomas paused. He sucked in huge draughts of air and wiped the sweat from his eyes. He did not want to blunder into the other Yankee.

There was sporadic firing up ahead, and every few moments someone screamed. But it was hard to tell who was doing the shooting.

'Mike,' the wounded man bleated, 'get the bastard! I can still see him … Mike?'

Either Mike had run off to leave his buddy to die, or he was out there in the mist, waiting for Johnny to make his move. Thomas would have laid odds that Mike was somewhere out there.

'Mike,' the man bleated, 'where the hell are you?'

Thomas was conscious of the hurried footfalls of other men as they rushed up the hill.

'Mike,' the downed man shouted, 'for the love of God, answer me!'

Thomas shook his head. Then, holstering his gun, he drew his knife and crept toward the wounded man. He paused just before he reached him, and, taking a deep breath, he sprang forward.

The man shouted, 'Mike … Mike, Johnny's at me!' And he struggled to fend his attacker off.

Thomas tried to end it quickly, but even with a belly wound the man was strong enough to grab hold of Thomas' wrist and grapple with him. Suddenly Thomas heard another sound.

He broke free of the wounded man, rolled off to one side, and threw the knife up at a shadow that was coming out of the mist.

The knife made a dull sound when it struck the ground. The shadow continued to come. Slowly, as the figure of a man solidified out of the mist, Thomas saw it coming at him with a bayonet.

'No more shootin' fer you,' the blue-belly growled. 'No more nothin'!'

'Get 'im, Mike,' the other one coughed. 'Get 'im fer me…'

Thomas slid away, trying to put some distance between himself and the blue-belly.

The man kept coming. He was a tall, broad-shouldered man with a full dark beard. Thomas' hand found the handle of his side arm. He eased it free and fired up.

The bullet smashed into the man's face. But he kept coming.

Thomas fired again.

The big man staggered. A low growl came from somewhere in the bloody pulp of what had been his face, and he dropped backward…

Thomas scrambled to his feet, picked up the Bowie knife from the ground, and then raced up the hill toward the hacking sounds of axes chopping into the obstacles in front of Fort Stedman.

Rifle fire was coming from the Federal side, but the thick swirling mist made it almost impossible for the sharpshooters to pick out and hold a target in their sights long enough to pull the trigger. The Confederates who were downed were hit by stray or ricocheting bullets.

The swacking bite of the axes devoured the wooden obstacles in front of the Fort, and there were cries urging the men who wielded them to work faster. Some of the

Confederate troops had succeeded in placing grappling irons on the palisade, and were already trying to scale it when Thomas reached the place where the axmen were splintering the outer defenses.

Confederate called to Confederate, each urging the other to break through so the others could get on with it.

Then the line was breached. The last of the timbers went down with a crash.

'Forward!' shouted one of the officers. 'Forward, men —'

A shot rang out, dropping the man in his tracks.

Thomas went through the opening. Several hundred Confederate troops were directing their deadly fire on the defenders, who fought back, but not with the same savage determination as the attackers. Many Union troopers fell in the first minutes. The wounded were screaming for help.

As Thomas fired into the thick mist where the Federate formed some sort of defensive line, he could hear their officers shouting commands, trying to rally their men and get them to hold until reinforcements came.

Flashes of flame darted out of the mist.

Some of the men in the Confederate line cried out in agony as they fell.

'Move out,' an officer shouted. 'Move out!'

The men went forward, but another line of red flames stabbed through the mist. A half dozen Confederate troops dropped to the ground. The others stopped.

'Don't let those blue-bellies hold,' a voice cried.

Someone gave the order to 'Fix bayonets…'

There was a pause, punctuated by fire from the Fort's defenders, and more of the attackers went down.

Then came the cry, 'Charge … Charge, men … Charge!' They rushed forward. Thomas ran with them.

Some of the Union troops stood and fired, but most of them broke and fled. Those who stayed absorbed the shock of the charge and closed in hand-to-hand fighting.

Men shouted and cursed. Men cried for mercy and were run through. Men were clubbed, trying to smash each other's heads while others jabbed, parried, and lunged in a deadly duel of death, a grotesque dance in which one partner always dies. Still others used only their bare hands to kill their enemy.

For part of the melee Thomas fired his gun until it was empty. Then, grabbing a rifle from a dead Union soldier, he swung it like a club, and beat a man senseless.

Howls of rage and screams of terror mingled with each other and drifted into the mist, now heavy with the sharp stink of burnt powder.

'We've got them,' a Southern-accented voice cried out. 'We've got them!'

Thomas surged forward. The enemy was still somewhere m the depths of the mist in front of him. Sweat poured down his face and soaked his clothes from the inside out. His throat ached from shouting, and his lips were dry.

'Keep crowdin' the bastards,' an officer urged.

From the number of men who lay dead or wounded, Thomas guessed that most of the Fort's defenders had fled.

Then someone in the center of the swirling combatants cried out, 'Surrender. We surrender. Throw down your arms, men. For the love of God, Johnny, stop the killing!'

Arms dropped to the wet ground, making dull thuds.

'All right,' a Confederate officer ordered, 'round up the blue-bellies and get them to the rear. Any one of them that runs, shoot.'

The Federals stood with their hands thrust high in the air while Confederate soldiers relieved them of their side arms and knives.

Thomas watched the prisoners being herded together. There were not too many of them. More lay dead than had survived. He reloaded his gun and then moved forward with the men who were going to capture the three forts behind Stedman.

More and more Confederate troops were pouring into the open area of the fort, and from some of the troopers came word that Battery Ten had fallen without a fight. So far General Gordon's plan was working perfectly. The artillery men who were in the initial assault were already turning the cannon in the Fort to fire on the Union's rear.

The slope behind Fort Stedman was much steeper than the men had anticipated, and it forced them to slow their advance. Some of the Confederate soldiers scarcely had any boots left. The rocky terrain tore through the thin leather and cut their feet.

Thomas silently cursed the hill and every damn Yankee on it, and wondered how the hell the men would have enough strength left to fight after —

The booming of several cannons thundered over the hills. Thomas looked down at Stedman. More cannons were fired, but the firing did not come from the Fort — or if it did. he could not see it because of the heavy mist.

Another deep-throated boom rolled over the hill. And moments later an orange-yellow flash erupted through the mist from the Fort below.

'The blue-bellies got the range!' a man exclaimed.

'Hurry, men,' an officer urged. 'We've got to get to those other forts.'

Unless the Confederates were able to win their objective and silence those Union guns that were shelling Stedman, the men there did not stand a chance of surviving. They pushed up the hill, forcing their will against their exhaustion.

Thomas suddenly realized that something was wrong. Some of the Federal troops that had abandoned Stedman should have given the alarm to the forts above. He quickened his pace until he gained the side of an infantry officer. 'Shouldn't we be drawing fire?' he questioned.

'They're holding back because of the mist,' the captain answered, between gasps.

'Seems like they should be —'

'Something's up ahead,' the guide shouted.

Any moment Thomas expected to hear the crack of Union rifles, but all he could hear was the loud pounding of his own heart and the crunch of hundreds of running feet…

They were at the wall, and then they were over it. But there was nothing there, nothing except some waist-high walls.

'Keep going, men,' an officer urged. 'This isn't it … it's still up a ways.'

The men raced fifty yards more up the slope, and another breastwork emerged out of the mist.

'This is it!'

Again the soldiers went over the wall, and flowed out into what had once been a gun emplacement.

'It's beyond,' shouted the guide. 'I can see it.'

'We sure as hell better find somethin',' one of the men yelled, 'or we ain't goin' to have anybody left in ol' Fort Stedman.'

'We'll take it now!' some officer yelled.

The troops rushed over the third wall. But there was nothing to take, nothing but weeds.

Exhausted, the men dropped in their tracks and listened to the sound of the Union artillery pounding Fort Stedman to pieces.

Thomas lay gasping for breath. The ground beneath him was wet from the heavy mist. He listened to the booming of cannon fire swell out and fill the predawn darkness. Minutes passed. A sudden chill gripped his body, making him shudder. He was cold now. cold not only from the touch of the icy air but also from the terrible ache of exhaustion. He and all those with him had pushed their bodies to the limit, drained them of strength and heat.

He looked at the prostrate forms of the men around him. He could see the faces of those who were close by. Some were bearded, some were young; all were smeared with grime, and all seemed to have a look of confusion on them. Thomas shook his head and silently cursed the men who had sent them on the mission. General Lee must have lost his wits and —

'Who the fuck said there were forts up here?' one grizzled trooper suddenly asked aloud.

'General Gordon —' began one of the guides.

The trooper snorted and derisively answered, 'You tell the general when you see him that ol' Hiram Danby pisses on him. You tell him that, you hear?'

A weary laughter rose from the men and, like a bird with a broken wing, quickly plummeted to earth. The men fell silent.

Thomas looked up. A gray streak was beginning to spread across the eastern sky. Soon it would be daylight. He pulled himself up and looked down at Stedman. Without the guns of the forts above it, the very best Lee could hope for now was to pull back and save as many men as possible. There was still too much mist down there to see anything clearly, but from the sounds that drifted up Thomas knew that a battle was beginning to take shape at Stedman. A battle, instead of a lightning-swift raid. And a battle was the last thing the broken Confederate Army needed.

He turned to the men. They needed the chance to live after having survived so much. He looked down the slope. Several smudges of black smoke were already pushing their way through the milky-white mist. If some were going to survive, they had to get down to Stedman. From there they would have a chance to make it back to their own lines.

Since he was the ranking officer, Thomas was about to assume command when a man said, 'You ain't thinkin' of leavin', are you, majer?'

Thomas wheeled around.

The man was grinning at him. 'Seems like you always get to be some place that you don't want to be. All of them don't want to be here either,' he said, gesturing to the men behind him.

'You're blocking my way, soldier,' Thomas said.

The man did not move.

Thomas stepped aside, and, walking into the center of the men, he began to order them on to their feet.

Few of the soldiers moved. But those who did were far more curious to see who was giving the orders than to obey them. Thomas could hardly blame their lack of response. All of them were experienced enough to know that General Gordon had sent them on a wild goose chase and —

'There be no more forts fer us'n ta take,' one old trooper said, ending his words with a squirt of tobacco juice from his mouth. The men agreed with him.

'None above,' Thomas said, 'but there's sure as hell one down below, and we've got to go back —'

'Shit, majer,' the same old trooper said, 'look at us. You think we're fit ta fight? We're plum tuckered out now from a-runnin' up this damn fool hill. We'll be in a lot worse shape if'n we run down again. I just as soon wait up here, rest some, an' see how the fightin' goes. I've never seen a battle,' he chortled, 'from a good place like this —'

'Elmer,' offered another soldier, 'has been too busy fightin' in them since sixty-one.'

'Suit yourselves,' Thomas told them.

'That's what we aim ta do,' the old trooper answered.

'I'm going down,' Thomas said. 'Those men who want to come with me —'

'I'll go, majer,' volunteered the man who had threatened his life.

'I didn't think that you wouldn't,' Thomas commented.

All of the officers and the three guides joined Thomas. Then some of the men changed their minds and said they would go too.

'Sooner or later,' Thomas said, 'the blue-bellies are goin' ta start blasting this hill.'

'I'll take my chances,' the old trooper responded. 'If'n it gets too bad I can always mosey on down yonder on da other side of this ole hill.'

'All right,' Thomas told those who were willing to follow him, 'we won't have any time to stop on the way down. The light is getting brighter, and the mist won't hide us.' He glanced over his shoulder. The Federal cannon had stopped, but the constant crack of rifle fire was coming from Fort Stedman. There was a good chance Union troops were counter-attacking and —

'majer,' called the old trooper, 'I don't want ya ta think I'm a-feared of goin' down and fightin' blue-bellies. But this war has run down an' I don't see no fool reason ta run it up again.'

'You do what you see fit,' Thomas answered.

'You don't give a man much leeway, do ya?' the trooper asked, using his rifle to pull himself up.

'Not much.'

The trooper sent a wad of tobacco juice flying and said, 'Guess I might as well see this damn war ta its end.'

A few more men changed their minds, and when Thomas finally ordered them down, less than a third remained on top of the hill. 'Keep going,' he told them. 'Just keep going … Even if you drop something, don't stop.'

Dawn had come and past. The mist was fast burning off the dull brown land, and the sunlight touched the leathery faces of the men as they hurried down the hill. They passed the old gun emplacement and in a matter of minutes were on their way to the first stone wall…

Once more Thomas was soaked with perspiration. The man who had vowed to kill him ran at his side. If he quickened his pace, so did the man. But there were whole moments — sometimes several in succession — when Thomas was able to forget about him, especially if there was a change in the sound of rifle fire, or if he lost his footing in a sudden slide and fought to regain it.

The men cursed as they ran. Many whose boots were torn left a trail of blood along the rocks and on the dead brown grass.

The first wall suddenly loomed up. The sound of rifle fire grew louder. Thomas was certain the Yankees had counter-attacked, and once they reached Stedman they would have to fight their way out.

The wall was just a few yards ahead. Thunder came rolling out of the distance, the booming thunder of a cannon. The men continued their dash down the hill. Then suddenly the earth shuddered and the wall rose into the air, stone by stone.

Thomas hurled himself down on the shuddering earth, engulfed by the screams around him.

Thunder boomed out again, but this time the Union shot found the top of the hill, devastating the former resting place. But there was no time for anyone on the slope to think about the torn, twisted bodies up there. The men scrambled to their feet without waiting for an order, and began running toward Fort Stedman.

The thunder followed them, shaking the earth under their running feet. They passed the blasted wall and rushed down the steep slope.

The Union gunners found them and filled the air with whistling shot. Earth spewed up in countless short-lived blooms of death.

Men were devoured by black bursts of earth. Some rushed through them while others dropped, screaming. Headless bodies ran for a few feet and fell. The slope, and the men on it, were being pounded to pieces by salvo after salvo from the Union guns.

Thomas ran. Instinct told him when to throw himself down and when to spring up and run again. Never had he experienced anything like the concentrated fire from the Union gunners. In a matter of a few minutes the slope of the hill behind Fort Stedman was plowed by Federal shot and seeded with Confederate dead.

With his brain numbed by the hammer-like explosions, Thomas twisted and dodged toward the fort. And always, keeping close to him, was the man who had vowed to kill him.

Then suddenly the Union guns stopped firing. The silence would have been deafening if it were not for the constant crack of rifles. Thomas slowed to a trot and then to a walk. He was inside Fort Stedman, or what was left of it. Confederate soldiers were too busy fighting off the counter-attacking blue-bellies. He turned and looked at the men who were coming in behind him. Less than half of those who had run the gauntlet had survived.

A haggard-faced captain approached him, saluted, and asked, 'Where in hell did you an' your men come from?'

'Up there,' Thomas answered, pointing to the high ground in back of the fort.

'After the blue-bellies got through blasting it,' the captain said, 'we didn't think anyone was left up there.'

Thomas was in no mood to explain what had happened, and after looking around he asked, 'Where are your men?'

'Those not killed or wounded are firing down at the Yankees.'

'But there were supposed to be reinforcements right behind—'

'They never showed,' the captain answered grimly. 'We came up after this place was taken, but none came after us. Seems like those bloody bastards took back Battery Ten. One of my spotters told me they're already fixing up to fire on us…'

Thomas looked at the men who had come down with him. They sat on the ground or stood nearby, waiting for him to tell them what to do. Of all the officers, only the lieutenant with the thin quavering voice had made it, but he looked like the trip had cost him his sanity. His eyes, as well as those of many of the men, were wide with a terror that would soon rob them of reason.

Becoming aware of the rifle fire again, Thomas turned his attention to the breastworks. Shaking his head, he asked, 'How many men have you got up there?'

'Sixty,' the captain answered, 'maybe seventy.'

'And wounded?'

'Twice that.'

'Dead?'

'I lost count,' he replied in a low voice.

Thomas looked down at the ground for a few moments, and then up at the sun. It was bright and shiny in a cloudless sky. He lowered his eyes to the captain and said, 'They'll take us —'

'Cap'n,' shouted one of the men from the breastworks, 'them Yankees are a-pullin' back.'

A triumphant yell went up from those troopers who had been firing.

'Get those of your men together who can run,' Thomas hurriedly told the captain. The tone of his voice made it clear he was giving an order.

'But —'

'If I were a Yankee general,' Thomas told him, 'I'd pull my infantry back and pound the shit out of the Johnnies in Fort Stedman.'

The captain nodded, turned, and immediately began to bark out orders.

When all the men were assembled Thomas said, 'There's a lot of open ground between here and our own lines. We're going to make a run for it. Don't bunch up. Don't give those Yankee gunners a good target. We might pull some rifle fire, and maybe mix it up hand to hand, but don't stop to fight unless you're forced to. Just run!'

In a matter of minutes the men swarmed over the breastworks and were on their way down the gentle slope to the Confederate lines. Their swift movement was quickly checked by Yankee rifle fire, forcing them to fight as they ran.

Thomas fired his revolver several times but did not pause to see if the men he hit were wounded or dead. He kept running down the hill. It seemed that he had been running all of his life. His throat ached and his legs felt cast in iron.

Here and there men grappled with each other, and thin screams of agony pierced the morning air.

Off to his side Thomas caught the glint of a bayonet. He paused, made a slight turn, and fired twice. The bullets struck the man, lifted him off the ground, and then flung him down like a rag doll tossed away by an angry child.

Thomas continued to run. Beside him ran the man who had been in the Yankee prison with him. Even as they raced down the slope, their shadows stayed close together, sometimes even melded with each other.

Suddenly there were no more Yankees in front of the Confederates. They had broken through the Federal infantry. But moments later the dark boom of thunder swelled into the sunshine-filled morning. And the long slope from Fort Stedman to the Confederate lines quickly became another Golgotha, where men gave up their lives on the bloody fragments of Union shot, where arms and legs were torn from their bodies, and where their screams of anguish were quickly flooded over by the continuous roar of cannon.

Thomas ran, and so did the man sworn to kill him. Then suddenly the earth spewed up a dark plume of death. The man faltered and fell to his knees.

'Oh, Jesus!' he cried. 'Oh, Lord Jesus!'

His own momentum carried Thomas past the fallen man, but he checked his wild dash to safety and rushed back to where the man was. 'Can you stand?' he asked, breathing hard.

The man looked up at him. 'You shouldn'a come back, majer,' the man told him. leveling his rifle at him. 'I'm goin' ta kill you.'

'Sure you are,' Thomas answered, 'but not now!' He drove his right foot against the rifle, knocking it from the man's hand. 'You can kill me later, or maybe the Yankees will do it for you.' And he scooped the man into his arms.

'You crazy son-of-a bitch,' the man shouted. 'You ain't never goin' ta make it with me.'

'I'm sure as hell going to try.'

'But why?' the other gasped, as blood came out of his mouth.

'Because — ah, fuck it!' Thomas exclaimed, and, tight-lipped, began to run.

'I'm bleedin' ta death,' the man whimpered. 'Dear God, don't let me die … have mercy on me!'

Thomas felt the slope begin to flatten out. The Confederate lines had to be less than a hundred yards ahead.

The Yankee gunners were still pounding the hill, though now and then a few pieces of Confederate artillery would answer. But the reply was weak. Weak the way Thomas was weak. His lungs pushed painfully against his chest for air while his heart pounded too loud for him to hear anything other than its beat. No longer had he the strength to make his legs obey his will. He slowed down, and saw that the man in his arms was spewing blood from his mouth.

'I can't run anymore,' Thomas told him, gasping for breath.

The man shook his head, and a moment later died.

Thomas stopped and put the body down. He never knew the man's name.

Hundreds of blue-uniformed men were racing down the slope. Without a moment's hesitation, Thomas started to run again. When he finally reached the outside of the Confederate breastworks, a soldier called out, 'This way. Hurry, this way.'

Thomas followed the sound of the voice and staggered into the sally port.

'We're pullin' back,' the trooper exclaimed. 'The general is already gone.'

Thomas nodded and said, 'He was never here.'

The soldier gave him a puzzled look, and with a shrug walked off into the woods.

Thomas drifted after him.

THREE

After the debacle at Fort Stedman, the Union Forces breached the Petersburg defense line and took the city on the second of April. The next day Richmond fell.

Lee and the remnants of the Army of Northern Virginia continued to fight, fall back, and fight again. But the army's death was so close that every day there were rumors that Lee and Grant were meeting to arrange for the surrender of the Confederate Army. And at night whole units deserted. There was even talk among some of the younger hotheads and the older officers of moving the troops to the west and fighting for the Confederacy there.

Never much of a talker, Thomas listened to the conversations of his fellow officers without making a comment. He could excuse the younger officers because they had tasted blood, some for the first time, and found it stronger than the strongest corn whiskey. But the older men had swilled blood for several years, and should have had enough.

As for himself, he had had enough. The action at Fort Stedman had been the final drink, and he was still gagging on it. His few hours of sleep each night were filled with wild dreams of himself and the other men running down the slope of Hare's Hill and never reaching the bottom. Running nowhere while the hill burst apart under their feet.

The sounds of cannonading in the dream often mingled with nightly firing of the Union batteries. When the two became thoroughly mixed, Thomas bolted up and found himself wet with sweat…

Afterward he would lie awake and stare up at the sky. Some nights he could see countless stars in the deep darkness. He knew the stars, and could use them to find his way. His father had taught him that.

And then he would remember how he had stood at his father's grave and Helen had said, 'It would not be unmanly for a son to weep for a father.'

He faced her. In a flat voice, and with his eyes narrowed down to slits, he said, 'I came home to kill the son-of-a-bitch. I'm only sorry that he didn't live long enough to let me do it.'

Those were hard words for a son to have said, and even thinking about them made Thomas uneasy. He knew that had he found the old man alive he would have called him out.

Sometimes, if Thomas was lucky enough to fall asleep again, he would find himself carrying the man who had threatened to kill him, and he would try to explain why he had left the column of prisoners. But the more he spoke, the heavier his burden became, until he was finally forced to set it down. The man died, but not before pointing an accusing finger at him.

The dream always seemed to end with the coming of the first light, and it left Thomas feeling more isolated from the rest of the men than usual. Knowing that nine of the ten men who had vowed to kill him might well get the chance did not make him feel any easier. Not that he was afraid. But he felt he had earned the right to move around without worrying about who was behind him.

One morning, with the dream still fresh in his mind and thoughts of the other nine men giving him an ugly feeling like a bad-tasting mouth after a hard night's drinking, Thomas joined the other officers to draw his ration of coffee and piece of hard tack.

'Well, major,' another man of the same rank said, 'looks like we might see some action today.'

Thomas cocked his head to one side and looked questioningly at Major Connelly, a scarecrow of a man with gape teeth, black hair, and a similar-colored mustache.

'We're being held in reserve,' Kiely, a captain of not more than eighteen or nineteen years, explained.

'For what?' Thomas asked.

'General Gordon is going to try and force the Federal front with his infantry, and —'

Thomas grimaced, set his metal coffee cup down on a crude wooden table, and muttered, 'He ain't fit to command a team of jackasses.'

The young captain's face flushed.

Still muttering, Thomas said, 'Only a jackass would attack now.' And he sat down, turning his back on Kiely and the other officers. The coffee was hot and bitter. He set the cup down and snapped off a piece of hard tack.

'We're reserve for Fitzhugh Lee's cavalry,' the captain said.

Thomas sat hunched over the table. He ground the hard tack between his teeth and then washed it down with a long drink of coffee. Though he heard Kiely, he had nothing more to say to him.

'Major —'

There was a flurry of movement behind Thomas, and some whispering. Then Kiely's voice rose above the others, and he said, 'By God, I've got a right to know!'

Thomas eased around.

Kiely shook himself free of the officers who were restraining him, and taking a step forward, he asked, 'Will you fight, sir?'

Thomas studied the man for several long minutes through gimlet-like eyes. Man? Really no more than a boy. Even his freckled face was boyish, and probably did not need to be shaved more than once a week, maybe even less. A shock of light-brown hair peeked out from under the shadow of a wide-brimmed but battered hat. The color of his hair matched the color of his eyes. Thomas had not noticed that before, and the discovery made him rub the heavy stubble on his own chin. Then he turned away and began to slowly chew another piece of hard tack.

'Will you fight, sir?' Kiely asked again.

The pitch of the captain's voice was like the whirring sound made by a bothersome bug, and Thomas reacted accordingly by waving him away.

Several moments of silence followed. Thomas took another drink of coffee; his thoughts were already beginning to drift back to his dream. But then he heard another officer say, 'I think Kiely is right. I think we all have a right to know whether Major Carey can be counted on if our —'

Thomas turned.

'Well, major?' Captain Kiely pressed.

'You're a damn fool, son,' he said in a hard voice, and went back to drinking his coffee.

There was some more shuffling behind him, and then several other officers sided with Kiely, demanding that Thomas answer the question.

Finally he stood up and, facing them, said, 'I'm not obliged to answer that question, now, am I?'

'As an officer and a gentleman —' Kiely began.

'I said it before,' Thomas said calmly, 'and I'll tell you again — you're a damn fool, son.'

The captain's face reddened, and he blustered, 'I suppose you think all of us are damn fools because we're still willing to fight for our country … I suppose you think that General Lee and —'

'Suppose,' Thomas told him, 'you stop telling me what I think and let me finish my coffee without asking dumb questions!' He sat down and picked up his cup.

There was another long pause, and before anyone could move or speak, the low hum of thunder came rolling out of the north. Union cannon were welcoming Gordon's infantry.

Thomas looked up at the sky — it was a lovely shade of light blue. Maybe there was even a hint of green in it. Some of the trees nearby were beginning to leaf. Again he rubbed his hand over the heavy stubble on his chin. As well as he could remember, it was Sunday, April 9th. Palm Sunday? He was about to turn and ask if it was Palm Sunday when Kiely said, 'The attack has started. Do you hear that, Major Carey? Those are Union guns. We may be called in any time now —'

Slamming the cup down on the table, Thomas was on his feet. He glared at the captain and strode away.

Kiely went after him.

'Have done with,' Thomas heard one of the officers caution. 'He's not one to keep snapping at.'

'Major,' Kiely shouted, 'I may be a damn fool, but there's been some talk about what your feelings are. Some of us are willing to go west and still fight for the South. You haven't yet said what you'll do. There's been some talk about how after Stedman —'

Thomas wheeled around so suddenly that Kiely stopped dead in his tracks. The damn fool kid was pushing him. Trying to make himself look like a man at Thomas' expense.

'If we go west,' Kiely asked, 'will you go with us?'

'No.'

'You mean you won't fight —'

'I have done my fighting,' Thomas answered.

'And if we're called to fight this morning —'

'Pray that we're not,' Thomas told him.

'Major! Stedman took the starch out of you.'

Thomas' hand dropped, and his gun cleared leather with such swiftness that it took the captain several moments to realize that he was looking down the long barrel of a .44.

'I've killed better men than you'll ever be,' Thomas told him, his voice like the snap of a muleskinner's whip. 'Now why don't you be a good boy and go west or fight or do whatever else you damn well want to do. But stop bothering me!'

Kiely's jaw went slack.

'And if I ever hear you mention Stedman again,' Thomas added in the same voice, 'I'll probably kill you. Now get!'

A murmur of disapproval came from the officers who sided with Kiely.

'What I said to Captain Kiely goes for all of you too.' Holstering his gun, he turned and walked away. This time no one followed. He went to his tent, where he rolled a cigarette and puffed angrily at it, thereby losing all the pleasure that came from smoking.

By late morning the order to mount up and be ready to move out was passed to Thomas' squadron. And when he moved to the head of his two troops, the troopers — who had heard what had taken place between him and Captain Kiely — murmured loudly among themselves.

'Steady the men down,' he told his two subordinate officers, who in turn passed the word to the sergeants.

When the men were quiet, Sergeant Saunders, a middling-sized man with a ready laugh and a firm but fair way with the men, rode to the head of the column. Saluting Thomas, he said, 'Begging your pardon, sir, but some of the men and me jest want you to know that if it comes to holdin' with you or Captain Kiely, we'll hold with you.'

A smile slipped across Thomas' lips, and he nodded. 'Thank the men for me,' he said.

Suddenly a rider came racing into camp. He reined in and shouted, 'The Yankees beat us off. Most of Gordon's men got trapped —'

'What about Fitzhugh Lee's cavalry?' Captain Kiely called out.

'A good many got kilt,' the dispatch rider answered.

'Well, what do we do now?' Kiely asked.

'We wait,' Thomas answered, and he ordered his own men to dismount and remain ready to ride, should they be ordered into action.

The rest of the squadrons were dismounted, and nothing more happened until just before noon, when another dispatch rider came rushing into the encampment with the news: 'General Lee and General Grant are meetin' at McLean's place in Appomattox Court House.'

To most of the men it was just another rumor, but some of the officers decided they would ride over to Appomattox Court House to see for themselves what was happening. Major Connelly asked Thomas to join them.

'Can't say that I'd be interested in seeing what's happening,' Thomas answered, 'but thanks for the invite.'

Connelly shrugged, and with the others he galloped off, while Thomas dismissed Connelly's squadron and his own. Now there was nothing to do but wait to find out whether Lee finally was man enough to face up to the fact that Grant had beaten him.

Thomas went back to his tent and rolled another cigarette; but this one he smoked slowly, enjoying it until there was so little left he could not even hold it.

Quite suddenly Thomas left his tent. Something was missing. Other men were standing outside their shelters too.

'The Yankee guns have stopped,' someone said.

Thomas moved away from his tent.

'It must be true,' an officer commented. 'Lee and Grant must be —'

'There's some of us who'll never surrender,' Captain Kiely yelled.

A number of officers agreed with him. But there were those who tried to tell him that the war was over. Kiely could not accept that, and angrily stomped back into his tent.

Late in the afternoon Major Connelly and the other officers who had gone with him to Appomattox Court House returned to the camp. Grim-faced, they rode slowly, and when they dismounted those who crowded around them waited silently to be told what they already had guessed had happened.

'It's all over,' Connelly said tightly. 'It's all over.'

General Lee signed the terms of the surrender. He was forced to clear his throat several times, and when he tried to say something more his thin face wrinkled up and tears streamed out of his eyes. The men opened their ranks for him, allowing the major to go to his tent without having to speak anymore.

All through the evening dispatch riders came into the encampment bearing news of the terms that Lee had agreed to. *All arms will be surrendered except the side arms worn by the officers … Men in the cavalry and artillery who own their own mounts will be allowed to keep them … Officers must sign a document not to take up arms against the Union again…*

The young hotheads led by Captain Kiely, together with the older diehards, spent the better part of the night discussing what they would do, but most of the men seemed more than satisfied that the slaughter was over. Some were even surprised that the Yankees were being so lenient.

'Excuse me, sir,' Sergeant Saunders said, coming up to the entrance of Thomas' tent. 'The men asked me to speak to you.'

Thomas motioned the non-com inside the tent. 'Sit down on the crate,' he told him.

The sergeant sat down, and after apologizing for disturbing Thomas, he said, 'The men want to know how you hold with the terms of the surrender?'

'They seem fair enough.'

Saunders nodded and said, 'It's the part about giving up our guns that bothers the men. Some of them do a powerful lot of huntin' … besides, we're not goin' to feel right without totin' our rifles.'

'What do the men want to know?'

The sergeant rubbed his chin. 'They were thinkin' that maybe you'd be able to tell them what to do?'

Thomas stood up, frowned for a moment, and then, with a smile, he said, 'When the time comes to give up your rifles and you're not here, you can't very well give them to anyone, now can you?'

'Guess not,' Sergeant Saunders answered with a smile.

'Remember,' Thomas told him, 'it's just a case of not being somewhere —'

'Yes, sir,' Saunders said, 'I understand.'

The two men looked at each other for a few moments, and Saunders saluted. 'Not too many officers like you,' Saunders said, 'and every one of the men knowed it.'

With a nod Thomas said, 'Good luck to you and to the others.'

'I'll tell them,' Sergeant Saunders replied.

Thomas watched the figure of the man until it vanished beyond the reddish-yellow glow of the campfires and disappeared into the deep shadows. Saunders was a damn good man…

Some time after midnight it began to rain. Thomas woke and listened to the drops drumming on the tent. That he would soon be going home seemed unreal and very hard to believe. He thought about the Broken Horn Saloon in Paso Diablo, the small town just a few miles from the ranch, and then suddenly his mind was filled with the memory of Lisa. He longed for her body again.

'But she's married now,' he whispered into the night. 'Married!' Thomas turned over on his side and said, 'And I'm married, too…' Then, shaking his head, he got up and rolled another cigarette. As he slowly smoked it, he wondered how he and Helen would get on.

It was raining in the morning, and colder. During the night the better part of Thomas' troops had drifted away. Alone or with them went Sergeant Saunders. Some of Major Connelly's men had left, too.

The war ended more quietly than Thomas had ever imagined it would. The men in the encampment spent most of the morning taking care of their mounts or readying their gear for traveling. There was little or no talking among them. Even Captain Kiely was silent. Whatever plans he and the others with him had hatched the previous night had been purposely kept a secret from the rest of the troopers.

At noon a colonel rode into the encampment with his orderly. He asked that the men be assembled to hear General Lee's last order. Remaining mounted, the officer began to read:

'General orders number nine headquarters, Army of Northern Virginia, April Tenth, Eighteen Hundred and Sixty-Five.

'After four years of arduous service marked by unsurpassed courage and fortitude, the Army of Northern Virginia has been compelled to yield to overwhelming numbers and resources.

'I need not tell the brave survivors of so many hard-fought battles, who have remained steadfast to the last, that I have consented to this result from no distrust of them; but feeling that valor and devotion could accomplish nothing that could compensate for the loss that must have attended the continuance of the contest, I determined to avoid the useless sacrifice of those whose past services have endeared them to their countrymen.

'By the terms of the agreement, officers and men will return to their homes and remain until exchanged. You will take with you the satisfaction that proceeds from a consciousness of duty faithfully performed; and I earnestly pray that a Merciful God will extend to you His blessing and protection.

'With an unceasing admiration of your constancy and devotion to your Country, and a grateful remembrance of your kind and generous consideration for myself, I bid you all an affectionate farewell.

Robert E. Lee
GENERAL.'

After he had finished reading, the colonel paused for a few moments before he said, 'Arms will be stacked on the twelfth of April. You will be told where to go.' He saluted Thomas and Connelly, and, touching the flanks of his mount with his spurs, he rode off, with the orderly following close behind.

Thomas turned and dismissed the men of his two troops. Connelly did the same. But none of the men moved. They stood in the rain. Thomas watched them. They seemed to be waiting for something, something more than the words that they had just heard.

Thomas nodded, and in a low voice he said, 'There's nothing more now, is there?'

The men shuffled uneasily, then one of them shouted, 'Well, fuck it, it's over and done with … and by the grace of God, we've lived through it!'

The men responded to that, and all of them began to talk at once. Thomas started back to his tent, and was joined by Connelly, who said, with a shake of his head, 'Lee sure didn't give the men a hell of a lot to hang on to.'

'About two dollars' worth, I reckon,' Thomas responded.

'You think Kiely and the others will go west and fight?'

Thomas shrugged.

'Could be the Confederacy still has a chance if we fight out there,' Connelly suggested.

'I wouldn't put any money on it,' Thomas told him.

After a pause, Connelly said, 'I guess not.'

They stopped a short distance from Thomas' tent and shook hands.

'You going home?' Connelly asked.

Thomas nodded.

'I'll go,' Connelly said, 'just after we stack our arms.' And then he added. 'Good luck, Thomas.'

'Good luck to you,' Thomas told him.

Connelly turned and walked across the open area toward a group of other officers.

Whether it was the result of his conversation with Connelly or not, Thomas could not say, but several hours later he had made up his mind to leave sometime that night. As far as he was concerned, he could just as well miss the stacking of arms. He was not about to give up his carbine, and since he was allowed to keep his side arm, staying around until the twelfth or even beyond would be a waste of time. By his own reckoning, Thomas felt that he had paid his debts, all of them. Even if men like Jason and the others thought that he still owed, he did not think that he did.

But when he was in the saddle and moving through the darkness, Thomas remembered one debt he still owed. And, changing his direction from the southwest to the northwest, he headed for West Virginia, to say goodbye to Jenny for the last time, since he doubted he would ever come so far east again.

FOUR

Soldiers from both armies moved through the long valleys and over the high hills of northern Virginia. The Confederates drifted south in groups of gaunt, silent men, while those of the Union Army too impatient to wait until they were officially discharged headed north. But there were those from both armies who chose to go west, having no better reason than 'it seems like a place fer a fightin' man ta be.'

Thomas traveled alone, seldom stopping to speak with any of the men he passed. He moved during the day, and when twilight came he made camp for the night, usually deep in the woods, where it would be less likely for him to encounter other soldiers.

One night, a week after he had left his unit, Thomas was sitting close to a small fire, over which he was roasting a good-sized rabbit. Except for the usual night sounds, everything was still. The sky was filled with stars, and Thomas was looking forward to having a good supper. Because two armies had lived off the land, game was terribly scarce, and this was the first time he had managed to bag a rabbit since he had begun to travel. Thomas hoped game would become more plentiful once he got closer to Jenny's place. He would have liked to bring her a deer, or maybe a wild pig…

That he would soon see her again brought a warm feeling to his groin, and made him wonder if she would let him…

His mount snorted nervously. Thomas raised his head and looked out into the darkness beyond the fire.

A branch snapped under someone's weight.

The sound was slightly to Thomas' left. Just beyond the light of the fire he saw two shadows. His heart began to race.

'Hey thar, reb,' a man called out, 'that rabbit smells mighty good.'

Thomas remained silent.

'Shame fer jest one fella to have a whole rabbit to hisself,' another man said.

'That's jest what I wuz thinkin', Gus,' the other man answered.

The two men came closer, and each had a rifle leveled at Thomas.

'Okay, Johnny,' the heavy-set one said, 'now up on yer feet an' keep your hands high in the air. That's right, reb … now jest step back a bit.'

'Hey,' laughed the other, moving into the circle of firelight where he could see Thomas, 'we've done caught ourselves one of those Confed's officers … now ain't that somethin'!'

Gus looked around the camp and said, 'He's got a mount that's a might more than some others have.'

The one closest to Thomas was tall and lean. He kept glancing down at the rabbit and licking his lips.

Gus moved over to the horse and said, 'Skin an' bones, mostly, but it'll fetch a price, an' he's carryin' the majer's carbine.'

'C'mon, Gus,' the one covering Thomas called, 'leave that blame horse an' get to that rabbit 'fore it burns ta a frazzle.'

Gus laughed and said, 'Don't you never think on anythin', Pete, 'cept grub?'

'Womens,' the others answered.

Gus went to the fire, hunkered over it, and looked at the rabbit. 'It's fit to eat,' he announced.

'What do we do wid the majer?' Pete asked. 'If'n we eat his grub an' take his horse, he ain't likely to be friendly toward us.'

Gus slapped his thigh and roared with laughter. 'Not likely a-tall,' he agreed. 'Not likely a-tall…'

'Seems like we got no choice, majer,' Pete said.

Thomas remained silent. His eyes looked past Pete and Gus. He was sure another shadow had moved just beyond the light of the fire…

'He don't seem much put out by the notion of dyin',' Pete commented. 'But that's maybe 'cause he ain't never done it afore.'

Gus went off into another fit of laughter.

'Majer,' Pete asked when his buddy quieted down, 'you been fightin' us fer long?'

'Some,' Thomas answered, watching for the movement of the shadow in the trees.

'Some, he says,' Pete said with disgust. 'Now what the hell kinda answer is that? I swear these rebel sons-of-bitches are all the same. None of 'em knowed nothin' about —'

'You expecting a friend?' Thomas asked.

Pete gave him a questioning look. Gus started to turn. There was a low whirring sound, followed by a dull thump.

Gus grabbed at his chest, trying to pull the knife out. He fell to his knees and screamed. Pete whirled around and fired into the darkness.

Thomas' gun leaped from the holster and roared twice. The first shot threw Pete backward, but the second one slammed him down on the ground.

With his gun still smoking, Thomas stepped over Pete's body and called out, 'C'mon into the light where I can see you.'

Nothing moved, but the shadow was still there.

'C'mon,' Thomas urged. 'I'm beholdin' to you.'

The shadow moved and a thin voice cried out, 'I'm hit … I caught one!'

Thomas holstered his gun and ran to help. When the shadow became a man he saw it was a Union soldier; a boy rather than a man.

'Where?' Thomas asked.

'The gut,' the boy answered.

Thomas carried him to the fire.

'Tracked those two bastards,' the boy gasped. 'They killed my friend just like they were fixing to kill you.'

'Don't talk,' Thomas told him.

'You got some water, Johnny?'

Thomas held the canteen for him.

'My stomach is on fire,' the boy complained.

'Maybe I could bring you to a town?' Thomas suggested.

The boy shook his head and then said, 'I didn't think I'd die this way … I mean, I've been fightin' for a year an' —' He gasped with pain and asked for more water. 'Listen,' he said. 'I got a sister; she's my only livin' kin … her name is Rose Mitchell. She lives in Sunflower Street in Cincinnati, Ohio. Maybe if you'll get up that way —' He stopped and shook his head. 'You really a Confederate major?'

'Yes,' Thomas answered.

'In all my fightin',' the boy said, 'I never saw a real major.'

'What's your name?' Thomas asked, wiping the sweat from the boy's brow.

'You ain't never goin' to Cincinnati,' the boy said with tears in his eyes. 'I mean, you're a reb —'

'I'll go,' Thomas said quietly.

The boy looked at him with big shiny eyes and said, 'Tell her that I didn't mean to cause her so much grief, tell her —' He started to cough, and blood gushed from his mouth. He died without finishing what he started to say.

Thomas went through the boy's pockets and found five dollars' Yankee money and a pocket knife. Not much to bring to his sister … not much for anything…

Thomas dug a shallow grave, and after burying the boy he marked the place with Pete's rifle. Then Thomas broke camp, leaving the rabbit smoldering on the spit and the bodies of the other two men where they lay.

Hours later, when the first light of day cracked the eastern sky, Thomas paused to rest his mount, reload his gun, and wash the bad taste out of his mouth with some water from a fast-running stream.

Late in the afternoon Thomas came out of the woods in back of Jenny's cabin and reined in. The log cabin was in front of him, beside a stream. It was from the edge of the woods that he had first seen Jenny, but there was snow on the ground then, and it was bitter cold. If she had not laughed…

Thomas stopped thinking, and nudged his mount forward.

No one was moving about, at least not outside. And even before he was halfway to the house he could see that the barn was in bad shape. The fence was down on one side of the pigpen, and —

He reined in some distance to his left. There was a mound with a crude cross stuck into the ground.

'Must be old Mister Lukins,' he said aloud, and rode close to the grave, where he dismounted. There was no name on the cross. Thomas shook his head and started toward the house.

Suddenly a shot rang out.

Thomas' horse reared, and he fought to hold him. 'Easy,' he said. 'Easy there, boy.' And then he shouted, 'It's me, Jenny … it's Thomas!'

Another shot came.

'You mount up,' a man yelled, 'or I'm goin' ta blow your head off.'

Thomas glanced back at the grave and then at the window of the house where the shots were coming from.

'Mount up, you Confederate sojer. Mount up or I kill you dead!'

'That you, Mister Lukins?' Thomas yelled.

Silence.

'Mister Lukins,' Thomas shouted, 'it's me, Thomas Carey!'

Suddenly a baby began to cry.

'Now you stop fussin',' the old man yelled into the house. To Thomas, he scolded, 'He wuz a-sleepin' fine till you come along.'

'Where's Jenny?' Thomas asked.

'Who are ya?'

'Thomas Carey. You remember me … I'm Thomas…'

'You come 'round front,' the old man said, 'an' let me get a look at ya.'

Thomas walked slowly around to the front of the cabin.

The door opened and Mr Lukins came outside, holding a shotgun. He looked at Thomas for a long time and then he lowered the gun and said, 'Jenny be wid da good Lord.'

A sudden stab of pain tore at Thomas' throat.

'You runnin' again?' the old black man asked.

'No,' Thomas answered, clearing his throat. 'The war is over.'

'You Confederates got beat?'

'Yes.'

The old man snorted with satisfaction and said, 'Best come in now dat da war is won.'

Thomas entered the cabin. The light was still good enough to see where he and Jenny had…

There was a baby on the bed, a baby the color of light coffee. He went to the child and picked it up. Its eyes were green, like his. From its size Thomas judged it to be a year old, give or take a couple of months. He turned to the old man and asked, 'Whose?'

'Damn fool question,' came the grumpy answer. 'It's Jenny's son … she name 'im John.'

'John,' Thomas repeated softly.

'I ask 'er why she give 'im that name,' Lukins said, 'an' she say it's fer somebody real special.'

'It was my brother's name,' Thomas said. He set the baby down on the bed again and told the old man that he would be back soon.

'Where yer fixin' ta go?'

'To Jenny's grave.'

'Best go b'fore it loses light,' he said. 'I'll tend ta da horse.'

Thomas walked slowly back to where Jenny lay. That John was his son, he had no doubt, but he was not prepared to find Jenny dead and himself a father — *That boy is mine,* he silently said, *and he ain't never going to be ashamed of what he is… he ain't never going to be ashamed because his mother was a black woman…*

Thomas came to the grave and looked down at it. 'It doesn't make sense…' His throat hurt too much for him to sound his thoughts.

He stood at the grave until the light slipped away and the long shadows of night crept over the land. Then he returned to the cabin and asked Mr Lukins when Jenny had died.

'She been sick since da baby come,' the old man said. 'She be gone now fer a spell...' His voice suddenly began to choke up, and he sobbed quietly. Then he told Thomas, 'I needs ta get milk fer John ... he ain't had no milk fer a spell.'

'Where's the cow and the goat?'

Mr Lukins made an empty gesture. 'Da winter's been hard an' I swapped 'em fer milk an' flour.' He shook his head and asked, 'How am I goin' get milk — how?'

Thomas looked at the child and then at the old man and said, 'I'm going to take you and John home with me. There's more milk there.'

'But this be my home!'

'You can stay here if you want to,' Thomas said, 'or you can come. But I'm taking John.'

The old man looked as if he were about to protest. But then he nodded and said, 'Jenny say you come fer da boy ... she say it before she die...'

Thomas put his hand on the old man's shoulder. There was nothing more he could do.

'What ya doin' up?' the old man asked.

Thomas had bedded down in front of the hearth. But he could not get to sleep, and as he lay awake listening to Mr Lukins' ragged snoring, he found himself remembering Jenny. He did not realize the old man had come up behind him.

He turned. 'I can't sleep. Not used to being indoors at night,' he told Mr Lukins.

'Can't sleep much myself,' the old man replied. 'Where's da place where yer takin' da chil' an' me?'

'Texas,' Thomas answered, going to the crude table and sitting down.

The old man joined him and said, 'Ya knowed I wuz a slave down in Carolina way. Me an' some others just run away … I come up here an' been here ever since. I got me a woman an' we jump da rope 'fore we got da preacher ta say words over us'n. Ma son Bob, he wuz born in dat bed. Bob be gwan a long time…' He paused and then, looking straight at Thomas, he said, 'I knowed fer sure he wasn't comin' back when you an' Jenny sleep in da bed togedder.' He nodded. 'I tol' her after ya left, she done da right thin' that way … I ain't never held bad feelin's because of it.'

'She was a good woman,' Thomas said in a husky voice. 'And when John grows up he'll be a good man. Now get some sleep … we've got a lot of things to get ready before we leave here.'

The old man retreated to his bed, and as he lay down he said, 'The Lord bless ya, Thomas, fer comin' back.'

Thomas said nothing. He stretched out on his bedroll, closed his eyes, and drifted off into a sleep filled with the sights and sounds of men killing and dying. Several times he bolted up, and often he cried out in his sleep…

He was up before the first light turned the windows of the cabin gray, and by the time Mr Lukins opened his eyes, Thomas already had coffee in the pot.

Thomas spent the next few days mending an old wagon and putting a tarpaulin over it to protect John from the rain and the heat of the sun. Mr Lukins would handle the wagon, since the mule pulling it was accustomed to the old man, while he would ride close by, most likely to the rear of it.

There were not many provisions to pack and load: a few sacks of flour, a bag of potatoes, a few pounds of coffee, a few pots and pans, blankets, the old man's shotgun and cartridges, and a couple of leather drinking bottles for John.

The day before they planned to start, four Union soldiers came across the creek and talked to the old man. Thomas was in the barn when he heard their voices, and was just about to call out to Lukins so the others would know there was someone else nearby when he remembered he had left his gun in the house.

The men stayed longer than Thomas expected they would, and all during that time he remained very still. Finally the men left, crossing the creek and disappearing into the woods on the other side.

Mr Lukins waited awhile before he came slowly toward the barn.

'What did they want?' Thomas asked as soon as the old man entered.

'Dey say,' he answered in a sorrowful voice, 'dat Mister Lincoln is dead. Somebody shot 'im an' kilt 'im.'

Thomas would never have imagined the old man knew who Mr Lincoln was, or that he would be affected by that man's death.

'Dat's a powerful bad thin' ta do,' Lukins said in a low voice. 'Seems like every time a white man becomes friends with a black man, somebody comes along an' kill one of 'em. Seems dat way fer sure…' He paused and then suggested, 'Maybe you an' da boy go widout me?'

Thomas shook his head. 'You're coming with me, Mister Lukins,' he said. 'Jenny would want it that way. Besides,' he laughed, 'the boy has got to know his grandfather.'

'Grandfather?' the old man asked in astonishment.

'Sure,' Thomas answered, laughing at his own foolishness. 'I just made you that.'

'Don't ya have a pa?'

Thomas shook his head, and for a moment he wondered how his father would have reacted to John. Most probably he would have called the boy 'the spawn of the devil.'

'Seems like I'm too black ta be kin ta you —'

Thomas shrugged, and with a laugh he said, 'Maybe by the time you reach Texas either I'll go toward your color or you'll come toward mine.'

The old man gave him a questioning look, and then, with a shake of his head, he commented, 'Now ya know dat ain't goin' ta happen.'

'Maybe not,' Thomas replied, 'but could you imagine some of the looks we'd get if it did?'

Lukins looked at him and started to laugh. Thomas joined him, and in a matter of moments they were slapping each other on the back to ease their coughing.

Traveling was slow, and the people who saw Thomas riding close behind Lukins gave them strange, sometimes angry looks. The roads were filled with discharged Union soldiers, making it seem as if the whole of Grant's army was moving with them.

At night, because of the wagon, they were forced to camp close to the road. Lukins would keep guard while Thomas slept, and then Thomas would spell the old man. After several days the rugged hills of West Virginia gave way to the gentle rolling country of Ohio. Now and then they would stop at a farm, and Thomas would offer to work in exchange for milk or flour or whatever else they needed. Sometimes he would work for money, earning as much as three dollars for the day. Most farms along the way were short of help, especially since it was time for spring planting.

Because he was still wearing his uniform, there was no way for Thomas to hide the fact that he was a former Confederate officer. Now and then someone would say something mean, but for the most part people seemed not to care that he had fought for the other side. And if he was angered by the ugly things a few said, Thomas never let it show. The last thing he wanted was to become involved in an argument about a war that, in his opinion, was best forgotten by everyone.

It was a good hundred miles between the Lukins farm and Cincinnati. With Thomas stopping to work, it took all of what was left of April and into the middle of May to get within a day of the city.

'By tomorrow night,' Thomas said to Mr Lukins, as they sat close to a small campfire, 'we'll be in the city.'

The old man nodded and said, 'I'll sho' 'nuff be glad ta stop sittin' on dat ol' wagon.'

'From what some of the farmers told me,' Thomas explained, 'we can ride down the Ohio River to the Mississippi and take it downriver to —'

'Seems like we'll be doin' a lot of downriverin',' the old man laughed.

'It beats the hell out of riding a wagon,' Thomas told him.

'Then I goes downriverin' any time you says,' he replied. He stood, stretched. 'John must be —'

Thomas saw the old man motion to him, and scrambled to his feet. Two mounted men were across the road. Each of them held a rifle.

'Kinda curious about you,' the older of the two said. 'I seen you back up the road, oh, round about noon yesterday is when I'd say you passed my place ... you stopped and asked my missus if she had any work around that needed doing.'

'Your place with the big white house set up from the road?' Thomas asked.

'Yep,' the man answered, 'that's it.'

'Ma said he was a Confederate from the way he talked —'

'Hush up, boy,' the older one said.

Thomas moved slightly forward and eased the old man behind him. 'Now just what are you so curious about?' he asked.

'Well, for one thing,' the man answered, 'that wagon. Seems like you take mighty good care of it.'

'That's a fact,' Thomas answered, knowing if he made a play for his gun either father or son would get a shot off, and at such close range he or the old man might get hit.

'You know,' the man said, 'there's lot of stories around about how some of you rebs managed to get hold of gold.'

'I didn't know that,' Thomas answered.

'Suppose you let us take a look inside the wagon?' the older man said, pointing his rifle at Thomas. 'Just move off a bit so my boy can see what you're taking such good care of.'

Thomas moved aside.

'The old man too,' the man said. 'I want to keep both of you where I can see you.'

Thomas called to the old man.

'Now just put your hands up,' the man said. 'That's right...' He nodded to his son, who dismounted, crossed the road, and climbed into the back of the wagon.

'Hey, Pa,' the young man called out, 'there's a baby in here.'

Suddenly John began to bawl.

'What's he done to dat child?' Mr Lukins grumbled.

'Just woke him,' Thomas answered, hoping the old man would have sense enough not to go charging over to the wagon.

'A baby, for real,' the young man said, leaping off the wagon. 'Couldn't tell for sure, but I think he's part black.'

The father must have wrenched his horse's bit, because the animal suddenly threw up its head and moved off sideways.

Thomas' right hand dropped. His gun leaped from its holster and, pushing the barrel against the young man's back, he said flatly, 'Stand easy, boy, or you'll die.'

The young man froze.

'All right,' Thomas told the astonished father, 'throw down your gun and get off the horse.'

The man did as he was told.

'Mister Lukins, get the horses and guns. Bring them around the front of the wagon and tether them there.' Thomas waited until the old man was finished. Then he said, 'Now see to the boy.'

'Just what do you aim to do with us?' the father asked.

'Teach you a lesson,' Thomas answered flatly.

'You going to kill us?' the young man asked, his voice quavering with fear.

Thomas snorted. 'Maybe I should,' he answered. 'But that wouldn't be a lesson, now, would it? No, I'm not going to kill you. I'm going to let you go. Just turn around and start walking.'

'But our horses,' the father protested. 'Our guns —'

'Walk!' Thomas ordered, and he fired a round over their heads.

Father and son turned and ran.

'If I see either of you again,' Thomas shouted after them, 'I won't give you the chance to run.' He holstered his gun and, sticking his head into the wagon, he told the old man, 'We'd be best off if we didn't spend the night here.'

'We goin' ta take their horses?' Lukins asked once he had harnessed up the mule.

'Down where I come from,' Thomas said, 'horse-stealing is a hanging offense. No, I'll send them on back once we get up the road a way. But we'll keep their guns. I think I'll ride up on the seat with you.'

The wagon moved slowly along the dark road. Sometimes they passed a farmhouse, its shape darker than the surrounding night and almost always set back some distance from the road.

The old man scanned the sky and said, 'Looks like it'll rain 'fore mornin'.'

'Seems so,' Thomas answered, glancing up at the clouds.

'You ever heard anythin' about gol'?' the old man asked after a long silence.

Thomas shook his head, then, realizing that he had not answered, he said, 'As far as I knew, we didn't have any gold. But there were some stories about how the blockade runners brought gold in.'

'Maybe,' Lukins suggested, 'if'n there's smoke there's fire.'

Thomas chuckled and said, 'This time I think there's a lot of smoke but no fire. After Grant got through with us, there was nothing much left to burn in Virginia.'

The old man scratched his head and asked, 'How come ya joined up wid them Confederate fellers? Ya don't —' He looked at Thomas. 'Jenny tol' me ya wuzn't like t'em a-tall.'

'Lots of things,' Thomas answered. 'And maybe nothing. I joined up … I guess that was the first mistake.'

Again the old man looked at him and asked, 'Did ya have feelins fer Jenny?'

'I had feelings for her,' Thomas answered in a low voice. He jerked his thumb toward the sleeping child. 'Enough feelings for her, Mister Lukins, to take John home with me.'

'And make me his gran'father,' the old man said with a smile.

'Yes,' John answered. 'Enough feelings for that too.'

The old man laughed softly and then called out, 'Gee'ap, ol' mule — I'm goin' ta Texas…'

FIVE

A cold wind-driven rain was falling by the time they reached the outskirts of Cincinnati late the following morning. The city was a busy place. The streets were crowded with all manner of wagons. Union soldiers were everywhere, and for the first time in more weeks than Thomas could remember he saw women who were soft and feminine-looking.

The people in the streets paid no attention to him and Mr Lukins, and he drove along the river front. After a while Thomas found a cheap hotel where a room for him and the old man would cost no more than seventy-five cents a night. He paid for one night in advance and then told the old man, 'I've got to get me some store-bought clothes … a pair of drawers, trousers, a shirt, and maybe a pair of boots.'

'Ya do what ya have to do,' Lukins answered. 'I'll take care of John.'

Thomas unbuckled his gun.

'I bet ya feels a might lighter widout it,' the old man said as he picked the child up and played with him.

'A might lighter,' Thomas replied, 'and a helluva lot less safe. But until I get rid of these army togs, I'm less likely to attract notice if I don't wear it.'

'Take care,' the old man cautioned.

Thomas nodded, left the room, and hurried down the steps to the small lobby. The clerk, a short, fat man, motioned to him from behind the desk.

'You got a baby with you?' the man asked.

'Yes.'

'That'll be another two bits,' the clerk said. 'The house rule is a dollar an' a quarter for three in a room … in advance!'

Thomas dug into his trouser pocket and fished around for the quarter. He looked at the clerk through narrowed eyes.

'No call to be angry,' the clerk told him. 'I don't set the prices here.'

Thomas said nothing, dropped the coins on the counter, turned, and went out into the rain.

In a few minutes he had found a clothing store, where he bought all the things he needed with the exception of the boots. He would have bought them too, but they were secondhand, and for the price they did not look as if he would get much wear out of them.

From the clothing store Thomas went to a barber shop that also provided hot baths for its customers. There he washed off all the sweat and grime that a month of traveling had put on him. Then he dressed in his store-bought clothes. Thomas had his hair cut and his face shaved close, leaving only a full mustache, turned down at the ends, the way the Mexican vaqueros back in Texas wore theirs.

The barber, true to the reputation of his calling, was talkative, and told Thomas that he could probably get a ride downriver for ten dollars. 'That'll take you to Cairo … but how far do you want to go?'

'Quite a ways beyond that,' Thomas answered.

The barber looked as if he were going to ask a question, but he said nothing.

'You wouldn't happen to know where Sunflower Street is?' Thomas asked.

'Sunflower Street,' the man chuckled. 'Sooner or later most men ask about it.'

'That's what I asked.'

'Just keep walking down this street to the public landing. It's off to the left … you can't miss it.'

When Thomas left the barber shop, his Confederate uniform was rolled under his arm. He walked to the public landing and quickly found Sunflower Street. But it was more of an alley than a street. It was crowded with men, and both sides of the street were lined with saloons. Drunks were everywhere.

Thomas went from place to place and asked the barkeep in each if he knew a Rose Mitchell. Usually all the answer he got was a shake of the man's head. But in the Screaming Eagle the barkeep seemed to hesitate before shaking his head. Thomas ordered a whiskey. The man was lying, and he watched him.

The barkeep set a bottle and a glass down. Then he said, 'You want a woman?'

'Miss Rose Mitchell,' Thomas answered, pulling the cork out of the bottle with his teeth. He poured himself a shot and said, 'I have a message from her brother.'

The barkeep looked at him with new interest and asked. 'Where you from?'

Thomas hesitated and then he said, 'Makes no difference where I come from … you jest tell Miss Mitchell somebody wants to see her.'

'You a reb?' the barkeep asked. His question drew the attention of the other men at the bar to the stranger.

'Listen, mister,' Thomas said, 'I come a fair way to give Miss Mitchell a message from —' In the mirror behind the bar he saw a woman. She was coming toward him. He turned. She was younger than he would have guessed, maybe his own age, give or take a year. Her cheeks were rouged, and her lips were colored red. Her hair was brown, and the low cut of her yellow gown showed most of her breasts, almost to their nipples.

'Stop gawking,' she told him sharply.

Thomas reached back for his shot and downed it. Then he said, 'I wasn't expecting —'

A sharp burst of brittle laughter cut him short. And then she asked, 'Now where is that no-account brother of mine?'

Thomas unrolled his gray coat, and, digging into its left pocket, he pulled out the small bundle of things he had taken from the boy's body.

Miss Mitchell looked at him questioningly.

'These were his,' Thomas said, handing the knotted kerchief to her.

She made no attempt to reach for it. Cocking her head to one side, she asked. 'How come you have them?'

Thomas was about to explain when a well-dressed man stood up at a table where there were two other men and joined the boy's sister.

'What is the trouble, Rose?' he asked, pushing back his brown velvet jacket to show the .45 Colt he packed.

She pointed to the stranger and said, 'Mike, that man says those things are Ed's.'

Thomas nodded. He was feeling more uncomfortable by the second. Everybody in the whole damn saloon was nailing him with their eyes. Even the piano player had stopped playing and was looking at him.

'Confederate?' the man named Mike asked.

Thomas set the small bundle down on top of the bar and, turning to the barkeep, he asked, 'How much do I owe for the drink?'

'You haven't answered my question,' the well-dressed man said.

'And I don't intend to,' Thomas told him, looking at Mike's reflection in the mirror.

'You're a cocky son-of-a-bitch.'

Thomas faced him. He went for his gun, but remembered he had left it in the hotel room. He checked the movement of his hand.

But Mike had seen it, and with a smile he said, 'Looks like you forgot something, eh, reb?'

'I didn't come here for trouble,' Thomas told him. 'I came here to tell Miss Mitchell that her brother is dead

'Ed is —?' she started to say.

'Yes,' Thomas continued hurriedly, anxious to tell her all and be on his way. 'The boy died in my arms. He said to tell you he didn't mean to cause you so much grief.'

'Oh, God!' Miss Mitchell wailed. 'Oh God, oh God!'

'And you come here,' Mike asked, 'just to tell Rose that?'

'Yes.'

The man pointed to the small bundle on the bar and said, 'What's in there?'

'The boy's things.'

'Throw it here!'

Thomas remained motionless. Tension was building in the place. He could almost feel it.

'I said, throw it here, reb,' the man ordered angrily.

'They belong to Miss Mitchell,' Thomas said quietly.

'And who the hell do you think she belongs to?'

'I reckon,' Thomas told him, 'that's none of my business.

The man took a deep breath and then he asked, 'How come Ed died in your arms?'

'He saved my life,' Thomas answered.

'He what?'

'The boy saved my life,' Thomas said loudly. 'He was gut-shot —'

'You shot him,' Rose suddenly squealed. 'You shot my brother.'

No one moved, and it became very quiet.

'Kill the reb bastard, Mike … kill him for me,' Rose hissed.

Prickles raced down Thomas' back. The woman must have taken leave of her senses…

Mike's hand started toward his gun.

Thomas leaped forward. Kneeing the man in the groin, he tore the .45 from its holster. 'No one move!' he ordered.

'Do something,' Rose screamed. 'He killed my brother an' now he's got Mike.'

With his left hand Thomas struck her across the face. 'Don't make me do that again,' he growled. 'Everyone over on the side,' he said, motioning to the left. 'You too, barkeep. I'm taking Mike with me to the door…'

Thomas pulled Mike to his feet, turned him around, and began backing toward the door, using the man for a shield. As soon as he reached the street he rapped Mike over the head with the gun and dropped him face forward into the saloon. Then, pushing the .45 into his belt, Thomas ran toward the public landing, quickly losing himself in the crowds of men.

By the time he came in sight of the hotel, Thomas had slowed down. Though the armies were finished fighting, the war would still go on.

He shook his head. Rose Mitchell and Mike would never have understood why he had come to tell them about the boy, even if they had bothered to listen to how a Union soldier had come to die in the arms of a Confederate major. Their kind could never know what the boy knew, young as he was, and what himself had come to learn through the long years of killing.

Almost as if his thoughts were heavier than he could bear, Thomas' body trembled…

By nightfall Thomas was fifty dollars richer from the sale of his mount and saddle, Mr Lukins' mule and wagon, and the two rifles he had taken from the farmer and his son. Everything was bought by the man who owned the livery stable across from the hotel. Thomas might have gotten a few dollars more if he had pressed for it, but he did not want to risk having the man change his mind because the price was too high.

Early the following day Thomas, Mr Lukins, and John — riding on the old man's back like a papoose — left the hotel and headed for the public landing, where they would board the river boat *Gloria*. They walked slowly, and several times Thomas asked if John was too heavy.

'He be light as a feather,' Mr Lukins said. 'Besides, if'n you carry him, people are goin' ta look more than if'n I carry 'im.'

There was something to that, especially since Thomas was now wearing a gun, with the holster tied down low on his right thigh.

'You ain't sportin' da same shootin' iron,' the old man commented.

'For an old man, you sure as hell don't miss much,' Thomas told him with a laugh.

'After a while I gets ta knowed da people I'm with.'

Thomas slipped his hand over the gun's butt.

'No need fer ya ta draw it,' Mr Lukins told him. 'I done seen it already. Where's da one you come from da fightin' wid?'

'John is minding it for me,' he laughed, reaching back to run his hand over the boy's small face.

The old man chuckled.

By the time they reached the ticket window, the night mists were rising off the water, and splashes of sunlight gave promise of a lovely spring day.

'All the way to Cairo,' Thomas said.

'Deck or cabin?' the agent asked, through teeth that were firmly clamped on the stem of a much-smoked corncob.

'What's the difference?' Thomas asked.

'Them that stays on the deck…' He looked at the passengers and then asked, 'He with you?'

'Yes.'

'That'll be the deck, then,' the agent commented, his hand going for the brown tickets.

'The cabin,' Thomas said.

The man looked at him suspiciously.

'The cabin,' Thomas said again, but this time there was a hardness in his voice.

'Five dollars each, for you an' him. The baby goes for nothing.'

Thomas paid, and with his white ticket in his hand he went off toward the mate waiting at the gangway, beckoning for Lukins to follow. 'Cabin,' he said to the burly man.

'Up them stairs,' the mate responded.

Thomas jerked his thumb back at the old man and said, 'He's with me.'

'Jest make sure he don't pester the passengers none,' the mate told him.

Thomas glared at him, and hurried the old man up the steps into the cabin.

'My, my,' Mr Lukins commented, 'if'n dis don't beat all!'

Thomas was still too angry to be impressed by the huge saloon, with its elegant tables, chairs, and sofas. 'I'll find a place for you and John to stay,' he said, 'and then I'll see if I can get us something to eat.'

The old man swung the child off his back and commented, 'If'n not eatin' puts ya in such a powerful distemper, ya should always eat 'fore ya do anythin' else.'

Thomas looked questioningly at him.

'I tol' ya, Thomas, dat most folks jest don't like seein' a white man and a black one —'

'I don't give a fuck what they like!' Thomas exclaimed.

The old man sat down and took John on his knee. Then, looking up at Thomas, he said, 'If'n somethin' happen to ya, then what happens to da boy?'

That was Lukins' way of telling him to bridle his anger. 'All right,' he said, heaving a deep sigh. 'All right.' Then he flicked his finger over John's nose, and, feeling much more at ease, he went off in search of food.

The *Gloria*, Thomas soon discovered, had a large dining room with white tablecloths on the tables, a good-sized bar that was already doing a thriving business, a place where a friendly game of cards could be played, and even several private staterooms where passengers could have not only the comfort of a clean bed but also enjoy the luxury of a hot bath.

Thomas returned to Lukins with a tray on which there was a pot of coffee, cups, rolls, a plate of hot sausages, and a supply of fresh milk for John.

The old man took care of the child's needs before he sat down to his own food, and then he handed a piece of roll to the boy to chew on.

Thomas told him about all he had seen. 'Go on, Mr Lukins,' he urged, 'walk around and see it for yourself.'

The old man nodded and said, 'Be better all 'round if'n I jest sit here an' let ya tell me about it.'

Thomas frowned, and a black anger rose in him that blotted out the golden light of the morning sun. He turned away from the old man and looked out on the river. On the Kentucky side there were willows all along the bank and —

'We be movin'!' Mr Lukins exclaimed excitedly. 'Oh, chil', we be on our way!'

Thomas faced him.

'To Texas,' the old man said.

'To Texas,' Thomas answered with a nod.

SIX

The *Gloria* swung out into the middle of the river, and with her stern wheel churning she headed downstream. Around one bend in the river, and Cincinnati vanished from view.

Hour after hour the steamboat followed the twists and turns of the river. Now and then the hoot of its three-note whistle boomed out against the rolling hills along the bank, and after a short pause it came echoing back.

The morning slipped away in the unbroken monotony of the river bank, though now and then Thomas would spot a deer that had come down to the water's edge to drink.

Sometimes he talked to Mr Lukins, telling him about Texas, the ranch, and the cattle, or he would play with John, knowing that even in their secluded corner people were giving him strange looks.

About noon the *Gloria* turned in to the shore to pick up a load of firewood that was already stacked on the bank. Thomas moved up forward with many of the other passengers to watch the black roustabouts heave the split logs from one to the other in a human chain. It took very little time to take the fuel aboard, and with three hoots of its whistle the *Gloria* backed away from the shore.

Before returning to John and Mr Lukins, Thomas stopped off in the bar. 'Whiskey,' he said, resting his right foot on the railing.

The barkeep put a bottle and a glass down in front of him and moved off to serve someone else.

Thomas poured himself a shot and downed it swiftly. He poured another, and took that one down in one swallow too. The third he let sit while he rolled a cigarette and leisurely smoked it.

The room was crowded with men, most of them wearing the uniform of Union Army officers, but there were some civilians around. Most of them were dressed in black and wore stovepipe hats. Practically all of the men, military and civilian, carried side arms.

None of the officers looked to Thomas as though they had ever been in a battle. They were too well fed, too well groomed, and their faces lacked the lines, the shadows and the tautness that killing would have etched into them. These men were innocent of all the horror that he and his Union counterparts had wreaked on each other.

Thomas picked up his third drink, and was about to down it when he heard a man nearby say, 'Now you know me, Sam, when I tell you something, it's got to be true. The rebs have a hoard of gold stashed away. And sooner or later some of them are going to try and bring it out.'

Thomas looked at their reflections in the mirror behind the bar. There were three of them — all civilians. Two were tall, and one of these was a bull of a man. The third was a medium-sized man, older and more dignified than the others. He said, 'Upwards of a million dollars was what I heard.'

'Closer to ten is what I heard,' the bull-like man said.

Thomas gave a low whistle. The sheer size of the numbers was enough to make his hand tremble.

The bull-like man whirled around. Glaring at the stranger, he growled, 'Did you say something?'

Thomas faced him and shook his head.

'Finish your drink, mister, and get the hell out of here!'

Thomas' eyes went to slits. He took the shot down, dropped six bits on the bar, and walked slowly toward the swinging door. Behind him he heard one of the men say with a laugh, 'If looks could kill, Bob, you'd be a dead man. That was one mean bastard there.'

The three men were staring at him.

Thomas paused at the swinging door, turned, and looked back to fix the image of the three men in his mind, especially the one named Bob.

The yellow light and blue sky of the afternoon slowly gave way to a soft twilight of high, feathery red clouds and lengthening shadows along the banks of the river.

The *Gloria* made another stop for firewood just before dinner. And then she moved downstream, the yellow from the lights on her decks turning the black water of the river golden.

Thomas sat, and as he watched the play of the light on the water he found himself wondering if there could be any truth to the rumor about Confederate gold. If there was any possibility that such a fortune existed, probably a great many men from both the North and the South were searching for it.

'Somethin' itchin' in ya head?' Mr Lukins asked, shifting John in his arms.

'Foolishness,' Thomas answered. 'Here, give me the boy. Hey, John! Hey there!'

The child giggled and made soft gurgling sounds.

'Sure looks funny,' the old man said, 'ta see ya fuss wid 'im. It sure woulda made Jenny happy if'n she coulda seen ya.'

Thomas agreed.

'I truly think he knows yar his pappy.'

'He sure as hell better,' Thomas answered with a laugh.

Mr Lukins shifted a bit in his chair and reached for the child, saying, 'Dat boy better get some sleep or he'll be fretful.'

Thomas handed the child to the old man, and quickly found his thoughts snared in a web of gold.

'I ain't never asked you…' Mr Lukins said abruptly.

'Asked me what?' Thomas responded, still thinking about the gold.

'You married up ta someone in Texas?'

'Yes,' Thomas answered softly.

'How she goin' ta take ta you bringin' —'

Thomas stood up, and, going to the railing, he said, 'I'm hoping she'll understand.'

The old man was silent for some time. Then he commented, 'I reckon dat's all we can do.'

Thomas put his hand on the old man's shoulder and said, 'I promise you, Mister Lukins —'

'Ya'll do what's right fer us, Thomas,' the old man said with a nod.

Thomas stood at the bow and watched the dark shores slide by. The chunking sound of the stern wheel intruded on the deep silence of the night. He was thinking of going to the bar and having a whiskey when he heard a low, breathy sigh.

He turned and saw a woman. She was leaning on the railing with her hands, and the river breeze was ruffling her hair.

'I couldn't sleep,' she explained to him.

Thomas had seen her several times during the day. Once she seemed to have been interested in John and Mr Lukins, but only from a distance.

He moved closer and answered, 'I'm afraid that's my trouble too.'

She was a well-built woman with an upturned nose and a pretty face. He guessed she was close to his own age.

'With the night so beautiful and still,' she said, 'I just couldn't stay cooped up in my stateroom.'

She smelled of lilac perfume.

'You're the man with the baby,' she said, looking at him.

'Yes,' Thomas answered.

She nodded and commented, 'He's a beautiful child.'

'Are you from around these parts?' Thomas asked, anxious to change the subject.

'No,' she laughed. 'I'm from back east — Boston. Ever been there?'

He shook his head. 'No, ma'am,' he told her, 'but I know about it.'

She looked at him questioningly.

'From the war,' he explained.

'And where are you from?'

'Texas.'

'Then you're —'

'A Texan,' he said quickly.

'Why yes,' she chuckled, 'of course!'

For a few moments neither of them spoke, and then she said, 'I'm going to visit some family in Cairo. Cousins on my father's side. This is the farthest west I've ever been.' Her voice took on a breathless quality. 'What I mean is that I've been to Europe and — You're staring at me!' she exclaimed.

Thomas' heart raced. He had not been with a woman for more time than he cared to remember. And this one was so close, so sweet-smelling. He glanced at her heaving breasts, and knew that she too was caught in a storm of emotions. He reached across the small space between them and put his hands on her arms.

Though she trembled, she did nothing to free herself.

'Where's your stateroom?' Thomas asked in a low husky voice.

'But —'

'Where is it?'

She pointed to its door.

'I'll be there directly,' he said, letting go of her.

She nodded, turned, and walked slowly to the door.

Thomas waited a few minutes and then went directly to the stateroom.

She came willingly into his arms and whispered, 'The walls are very thin.'

He nodded and ran his hands over her body.

'Wait,' she told him, and turned down the light.

Thomas took her in his arms and put his lips to hers. In a very few minutes they lay naked in each other's arms.

'I know,' she said as his hands caressed her breasts and her bare belly, 'that you —'

Thomas did not want to hear what she started to say. He only wanted the pleasure her body could give, and for that words were not necessary. He stopped her from speaking with a kiss, and, rolling over her body, he coupled with her.

As he moved, she moved. Her moans of delight were low and came from deep in her throat. When her moment of pleasure came she rolled high on her back and wrapped her naked thighs tightly around his bare back. With a low growl of animal pleasure, Thomas' own passion came roaring out of his body.

Spent, they lay naked in each other's arms until Thomas stroked her to readiness again. He took her once more. This time there was a violence to their coupling.

Just before the first light, Thomas left the woman's stateroom. He had not asked her name, and she had not inquired after his. Sometimes things like that happened between a man and a woman, and when they did, names were not necessary. But Thomas felt she had lain with him because he had been a rebel soldier.

He gave a snort of disdain. If that had been her reason, it was a damn strange one.

The day dawned gray, and there was the threat of rain in the air. The *Gloria* came alongside the landing in Cairo at eight o'clock in the morning. By that time a thin drizzle was already falling.

Thomas tried to see the woman with whom he had spent most of the night, if for no other reason than to say goodbye. But when he did see her, she looked at him for a moment, nodded, and then, turning away, went toward the stairway.

Realizing the woman wanted no further connection with him, Thomas made no attempt to follow. He immediately went about the business of getting John and Mr Lukins ready to disembark. The old man was in a sulky mood, mumbling to himself all during the time it took them to leave the *Gloria* and purchase tickets for the trip down to Memphis on the *Anita G.*

'This time,' Thomas told Mr Lukins, hoping it would cheer him up, 'I got you and John a stateroom.' He was sure the old man's sulks were the result of having to spend the night in a chair.

'No need to waste ya money like dat,' Lukins told him.

'You'll sleep better,' Thomas said as they boarded the *Anita G* and made their way upstairs to the cabin deck. The saloon on this steamboat was much larger than the one on the *Gloria*. It was also more lavishly decorated.

'I sleep good 'nuff. I sleep good 'nuff ta knowed dat ya wuz tomcattin' roun' wid a pussy —'

'That's enough!' Thomas said sharply. The man was taking liberties.

The old man's jaw went slack and began to tremble. But he kept silent.

'Listen,' Thomas told him when they reached the stateroom, 'I'm damn sorry I let fly at you. But I'm not a saint —'

'You be married up,' the old man said.

'All right,' Thomas answered, 'then what about Jenny and me? I was just as married then as I am now.'

Mr Lukins nodded. 'Ya had feelin' fer her,' he said. 'Feelin' 'nuff to come back.'

'Old man,' Thomas told him in a low angry voice, 'I'm a man and I need what a man needs from a woman. But what I do with any woman, or anything else, is none of your damn business!'

Mr Lukins' jaw was trembling. Tears streamed down his dark cheeks. 'I don't want ya ta get hurt,' he sniffed. 'If'n ya sin, da hand of da Lord be agin ya, Thomas, an' I don't want dat. Lord, I don't want dat ta happen to ya!'

Thomas shook his head. What could he say to the old man?

Lukins sank down on the bed, his body wracked by half-stifled sobs.

'I'm not angry anymore,' Thomas said with a sigh.

The old man looked up.

'C'mon,' Thomas told him, 'we'll get us some breakfast.'

'Ya sure 'nuff not angry with me?'

'Sure enough,' Thomas answered.

The old man blew his nose and wiped his eyes. 'I ain't goin' mess wid ya tomcattin' ever agin. If ya needs ta tomcat, then da good Lord must have his hand in it some way or t'other.'

Thomas smiled and said, 'That's sure an interesting way of looking at it. I wish my old man would have seen it that way.'

'Granddaddies have special ways ta look at thin's,' Lukins said, standing up and taking John in his arms. 'Now don't dey, boy?'

The child giggled happily.

It took the better part of two days and three nights for the *Anita G* to make the trip from Cairo to Memphis. The Mississippi River seemed wider to Thomas than the Ohio, but not much more interesting. There was nothing to do aboard, except eat, drink, sleep, and play cards. Thomas took advantage of all four, and by the time the *Anita G* made fast to the landing in Memphis, he had won five hundred dollars in gold by playing poker.

After a few hours in Memphis, Thomas booked passage on the *Jefferson* to Vicksburg. From there he planned to go west across Louisiana and into Texas.

At four o'clock in the afternoon the whistle from the *Jefferson* blew three long blasts, the roustabouts slipped the lines free, and the big steamboat began to chunk its way downstream.

Aboard there were many other Southern men, most of whom, like Thomas, had fought in the Confederate Army. They were going home, and even if they had money for the cabin class, they were gaunt, hollow-cheeked men with a strange faraway look in their eyes. Many still wore their threadbare grays, and most needed boots. For the most part they preferred to remain alone or, if they did congregate together, it was never more than two or three of them. Though they were beaten, they still possessed a fierce pride that made the Union troops on board keep their distance.

These defeated men quickly recognized Thomas as one of themselves. But when they saw him with John and Lukins, their faces filled with confusion and then became twisted with hate. He met their looks of silent anger with an equally silent challenge that none was willing to accept.

After John and Lukins were asleep, Thomas left the stateroom and went into the saloon, with the hope of sitting in on a poker game for a few hours. Only three games were in process, and from the way they were going, it seemed unlikely that any of the players would soon quit his place at the table.

Thomas went to the bar and ordered a whiskey. He had just finished pouring himself a drink when he saw their reflections in the mirror. There were six of them fanned out in a semicircle behind him.

Thomas set the bottle down on the top of the bar and eased himself away.

'As soon as I got told about some reb with a nigger and a nigger chil',' a tall man said, 'I got the feeling that it might be the same kind of son-of-a-bitch I knew in a Yankee prison camp.'

Thomas stiffened.

'Turn around so I can get a good look at you.'

'Who are you?' Thomas asked, trying to keep the choked-up sound out of his voice.

'Mason,' the man answered. 'Horace Mason.'

There was a long pause. The other customers moved off to one side. Even the Union officers eased away.

Thomas studied the reflection of the man's face, hoping that he would remember it. But it was too much like a host of other gaunt, hollow-cheeked faces he had seen. It was even like his own, except that Mason was bearded.

'Turn around, Lieutenant Thomas Carey. I want to see your face when you die.'

Thomas did not move.

'Face me, you bastard!' Mason shouted. 'I want to see —'

A sudden gasp cut him short.

Even as he spun around, Thomas' hand slapped leather. But he did not fire.

Mason looked down the Colt's long barrel.

'We'll both die,' Thomas said flatly.

'I have a score to settle with you.'

'It's not worth it.'

'Call him out, Mason,' one of the men in the semicircle suggested. 'Either that or stop jawing about how you're going to kill —'

'Somebody say when,' Mason said, holstering his gun.

One of the men volunteered.

'You're a fool, Mason,' Thomas told him. 'You're a damn fool.' He slipped his gun back into the holster.

Mason stood at one end of the bar, Thomas at the other.

'Start counting!' Mason said.

'I don't want this fight,' Thomas told him.

'The men you left to die,' Mason answered, 'didn't want to die. Start the count.'

'Okay,' the man said. 'I'll go to three. Ready?'

As the 'three' came out of the man's mouth, Thomas' gun leaped into his hand. A single shot exploded.

The slug slammed into Mason, doubling him up. He dropped to the floor, screaming in agony. Gut-shot, he would scream for a long time before he died.

Thomas stood over Mason and looked down.

'One of the others will kill you,' Mason gasped. 'One of the others will get you, Carey.'

'Maybe,' Thomas answered. 'Maybe.' He shook his head, holstered his gun, and walked slowly out of the bar without looking at anyone. 'The fool,' he whispered. 'The stupid fool.' But he knew there were eight more just like Mason who had sworn to kill him.

He shrugged. There was nothing he could do, except — when the time came — face them and fight for his life.

Late the following morning the *Jefferson* reached Vicksburg. Thomas bribed the mate with a five-dollar gold piece to let him, John, and Lukins leave the steamboat before any of the other passengers.

'I'm sure happy we be finished with river boats,' the old man said as they hurried away from the wooden landing and up a street lined with smashed and fire-gutted buildings.

'So am I,' Thomas agreed. 'But I'll feel a lot better once I have a horse under me and we're away from here.'

Two hours later Thomas was in the saddle of a big bay and Mr Lukins rode a gray mare. Neither horse was anywhere near top quality, but they were the best Thomas could buy. By nightfall Thomas and the old man were several miles south of Vicksburg, and made camp.

'You sleep first,' Thomas told Lukins. 'I'll wake you in a few hours.'

Using his saddle for a head rest, the old man stretched out, and, drawing a blanket over himself, he said, 'Goodnight.'

Thomas nodded. In a short time the old man was snoring loudly.

Thomas rolled a cigarette, and, resting his back against his saddle, he wondered how he was going to explain John and Lukins to Helen. It was getting close to the time when he would have to think of something, something that she might believe.

Helen was harder than when he'd married her. Almost flinty in a way. She kept the ranch going — that much he would give her credit for.

But how would it be between them? Thomas admitted that he had never had much feeling for her as a woman, and she had been too damn taken up with being good in the eyes of God to have been worth a damn in bed.

Suddenly he was filled with the old bitterness and the all-too-familiar ache of loving one woman and being married to another. Lisa sprang into his thoughts. Lisa, the Mexican girl, whom he had loved and who had loved him. She was married now, to the blacksmith in Paso Diablo.

Thomas heaved a deep sigh and looked up.

The sky, a dark blue expanse, was filled with stars. He nodded appreciatively and told himself, 'It's still good to be going home. Good to be alive.'

SEVEN

The next morning it rained. But Thomas, impatient to be moving, broke camp and led Mr Lukins south along the Mississippi. At noontime they crossed the river on a makeshift ferry worked by two sullen-looking men, who controlled the movement of the raft with long sweeps.

For three days and as many nights the rain continued, turning the low flatland of Louisiana into a sea of mud. But despite the downpour, the old man managed to keep the baby dry.

They moved from dawn to dusk and found shelter for the night wherever they could. Sometimes they came across burnt-out houses or barns. Using part of what was left of them, and a piece of canvas, Thomas managed to make a fairly good lean-to.

During the day they passed squads of mounted troopers and civilians who moved along the road in both directions. They were sullen-looking. The fields that once had been given over to the raising of cotton, sugar cane, and other crops were now fallow.

On the fourth day the rain stopped, though the sky remained overcast with dark gray clouds. But the next morning the sky was a lovely blue, and the sun was delightfully hot.

Two weeks after they had crossed the Mississippi, Thomas told Mr Lukins, 'We're in Texas.'

'Sure don't look no different from where we wuz.'

Thomas assured him that before they reached the ranch the land would look very different from anything he had ever seen.

Thomas lost count of the days that passed. By the time they crossed the Brazos and the Colorado, spring had ripened into summer. The land was parched and scarred with gullies. The green lushness of east Texas gave way to brown range grass, tumbleweed, brush, and stunted trees. Traveling became harder, and because the horses were almost worn out, they were forced to slow their pace. But nothing that happened brought a word of complaint from the old man.

There were a great many strays on the range, and more than once he saw the charred ruins of a ranch house or crossed the trail of a party of Indian braves.

Now and then they would meet up with a drifter, and the story would always be the same: 'If'n the injuns don't burn ya out, then some guns come along an run ya off. I seen it happen a dozen times way out ta the Pecos.' Some of the drifters were just ranch hands. Others were ranchers with a couple of hundred head of their own. All of them counseled Thomas to turn back.'

Thomas thanked them for their advice and continued on his way. Though Mr Lukins, who was always in earshot of these conversations, never said a word about them after the rider left, Thomas always felt a bit peculiar. The months he had spent with the old man had brought them close together as men, and until someone reminded Thomas, he always forgot the old man was black.

Often while they were in the saddle or sitting at the campfire, Thomas spoke to Mr Lukins about his brother John, who fought for the North and was killed in a Confederate prison; and about Clem, who was a Confederate officer and was reported missing at Chickamauga.

The old man listened., and sometimes spoke about his days as a slave, or his wife. But mostly he spoke about his son Bob.

'Ya would-a gotten on fine wid him,' he told Thomas one night. 'Ya like him. Dat's why Jenny take ye to her bed.'

'I would have liked him,' Thomas answered, playing with his son. 'Especially if he was like you, Mister Lukins.'

The old man laughed and said, 'Ya suppose ya knowed me well 'nough to call me Jethro, seein' as how I'm John's granddaddy.'

'Jethro?' Thomas questioned.

'Seems like I remember that be my daddy's name. But he wuz sold, an' I never did get ta know him.'

'All right, Jethro,' Thomas said. 'I think I know you well enough to call you that.'

'Better give me John,' Jethro told him, 'or you'll be playin' wid him all night.'

Thomas handed the child to the old man, and then put several more pieces of wood on the fire.

'Aren't ya goin' to turn in?' Jethro asked, once he had put the baby to sleep.

'I'll sit awhile,' Thomas answered.

The old man nodded and, stretching out, pulled a blanket over himself.

Thomas rolled a cigarette, lit it with a glowing ember, and enjoyed the taste of the smoke. He was bothered by the stories the drifters were telling him. Indians were trouble enough: the ranchers did not need additional trouble from hired guns. Well, in a few days he would be home, and then he would find out for himself what had been happening. He flicked the tip off the cigarette and put the rest of it in his jacket pocket, to finish after coffee in the morning. He stretched out and used his saddle for a head rest.

The following day they rode until mid-afternoon. Then Thomas called a halt near a creek, more to rest and water the horses than anything else, because in front of them lay several miles of rough hilly country.

'Once we're on the other side of them,' Thomas explained, 'the country flattens out again.'

'Think we'll make it by sundown?' Jethro asked as he took John and washed him in the creek.

Thomas shrugged and said, 'I don't want to push the mounts too much.' He gathered some wood, made a fire, and had coffee boiling by the time Jethro was finished with the baby.

'How come,' the old man asked as he drank his coffee and chewed on a piece of hard tack, 'ya never talk about ya pa or 'bout your woman?'

'There's nothing to say about them,' Thomas answered.

'Dere's somethin' ta say 'bout everybody,' Jethro told him. 'But if'n ya don't want ta, ya don't have ta.'

Thomas nodded and remained silent. But just before they mounted up, he said, 'My pa is dead and it doesn't make much sense to rehash the trouble that was between us.'

Jethro agreed.

'And as for my wife,' Thomas explained, 'she's a good —' He stopped. Way out where the sky and the earth touched each other, he saw two riders.

'Don't fret none 'bout it,' Jethro said, 'some peoples like ta talk an' some peoples don't. Yer not da talkin' kind.'

The two riders were not moving. But Thomas was sure that if he could see them, they could also see him.

'You lookin' at somethin'?' Jethro asked, turning around to scan the parched brown land.

Thomas shook his head; there was no reason to worry the old man.

The riders were trailing them. He wondered who they were and what they wanted. They might be Indians, but they could also be scavengers. Either of them would be damn hard to handle with the boy and the old man to protect.

For the rest of the afternoon Thomas led Jethro rapidly along the trail. He wanted to be out of the hills by nightfall. But his mount could not hold the pace. Finally Thomas stopped.

'What's wrong?' Jethro asked.

'Nothing,' Thomas told him. 'I wanted you to see some landinos in the brush there. They're about as wild as they come.' He stood up in his stirrups to look for the riders. They were nowhere in sight. He would have felt much better if he had seen them.

'How far we got to go?' the old man asked when they began to move again.

'Two, maybe three, days at the most.'

'Fer sure?'

'For sure.'

'I wuz glad ta leave da river boat, but I be more gladder ta get off dis horse.'

'It's been a long ride,' Thomas said, 'there's no doubt about that.'

'But soon we be in da promis' lan'!' Jethro exclaimed, swinging his mount alongside of Thomas'.

Thomas started to laugh, but the glint of blue metal in the late-afternoon sun stopped his laughter. His gun leaped from the holster. He spurred his mount and rushed forward. A shot exploded from the long gray shadows.

Thomas saw the glint of the rifle barrel again. He threw two shots at it. A man screamed.

He fired again. A figure crouching low in the saddle suddenly broke from the side of the hill and made a run for it.

Thomas cut to the side. The second man lay face up with two slugs in his chest.

'Why?' Thomas shouted.

But the man was dead.

Thomas turned and raced back to Jethro. The old man was slumped over in the saddle, with blood pouring out of his stomach.

'Take John,' the old man said. 'Don't let 'im fall.'

Thomas lifted the old man off the horse and slipped the baby from his back before setting the old man down on the ground.

'I ain't never goin' ta get ta da promis' lan',' Jethro said. 'I ain't —' He died without finishing what he started to say.

Thomas closed the old man's eyes. He buried Jethro off to one side of the trail, and placed rocks on the shallow grave to keep the wolves and coyotes away from the body.

He went back to the dead gunman. Nothing on his person identified him.

Thomas took the dead man's mount and led it back to where his own was. Then he strapped John to his back, mounted up, and, looking down at the mound for the last time, Thomas whispered in a choked voice, 'Goodbye, Grandfather, goodbye.' He rode off with two riderless horses in tow.

EIGHT

Thomas rode all night. The moon was full and very white. He passed north of Paso Diablo and turned toward the ranch. By the time the moon had set, he had topped the ridge. The dark, low mass of the ranch house was below at the end of a long slope.

Thomas reined in, swung out of the saddle, and removed John from his back.

'We'll rest here for a while, boy,' he said, holding the child close to him. 'There's no sense in rousing everyone. The sun'll be up soon, and then we'll go riding in.'

He set the baby down against a large rock and rolled a cigarette. As soon as it was lit, he drew a blanket from his saddle pack, and, placing it around his shoulders, Thomas sat down next to the child.

'Once I get you fixed up, John, and rest some myself,' he said to the baby, 'I'm going to take that gunman's mount and go into Paso Diablo. Maybe someone there will be able to tell me who owned him.'

The boy made several gurgling sounds.

'Don't you fret none,' Thomas told him. 'I'm going to get the *hombre* who bushwhacked your granddaddy. You know, you couldn't have picked a better granddaddy if you tried.'

He smoked in silence for some time and watched the pre-dawn darkness fade in the east.

'We'll be riding in soon,' Thomas told the child. 'You've got to be extra good when you meet Helen. And you've got to give her some time to get used to you.' He stamped out his cigarette against the dry earth. 'It's not the same as us, son,' he explained, lifting the child in his arms. 'We got blood between us.' He nodded at what he had just said. 'But don't worry, John, don't you worry about a thing.'

Thomas drew the blanket around the baby and waited. When the sky in the east flushed, he mounted up and rode slowly toward the ranch house.

He saw that the fence needed mending. And long before Thomas came close to the front yard, the dogs barked furiously. He rode up to the gate and started to unhitch. 'Just stay where you are, mister, or I'll —' a woman cried out.

'Helen, it's me, Thomas!' he shouted.

'Thomas?' she yelled. 'Oh my God, Thomas … Thomas!' And, still holding the rifle, she came running out of the half-light of the doorway.

He opened the gate and dismounted, leading the three horses into the front yard. She looked thinner to him. As she ran her long blonde hair flew back, revealing the ugly scar on the right side of her neck where Zeb had cut the muscle, making her head flop off to the right. If that had never happened to her, she still would have been a good-looking woman. But watching her head bounce as she ran made Thomas wince. That he had been responsible for what had happened, he could never deny. Responsible for the way she had been raped and cut. He stopped and tried to clear the past from his mind.

Helen slowed down. The closer she came to him, the more uncertain she became. Finally, when she was just a few paces from him, she stopped. Her hand immediately flew to her hair. She moved it over the scar.

Thomas flushed and said, 'I'm glad to see you, Helen.'

She nodded and said, 'Welcome home.' Her eyes moved past him.

Thomas slipped John off his back.

'What are you doing with that baby?' Helen asked.

'Found him,' he said, looking straight at her. The words came so easily that he wondered if he had thought of them before. 'I found him on the trail back a ways.'

'Found him?' she repeated, turning his statement into a question.

Thomas nodded.

'But how?'

'People move all over the place now,' he said. 'His daddy or maybe his granddaddy was bushwhacked, I guess. Anyway, he was dead when I got to him, and there was this baby —'

'And the horses, too?' Helen asked.

'Yes.'

'Seems like one is a cow pony and the other —'

'Eastern stock.'

'How could they come by a cow pony?'

Thomas shrugged.

Her blue eyes bored into him.

After a long pause Helen said, 'Give him here.' She handed the rifle to Thomas and took the child from him. 'From the size of him, I'd guess he's past a year. Looks healthy.'

Thomas tethered the horses at the hitching post and then, as they went toward the house, he put his arm around her shoulders.

Helen glanced at him and said, 'I prayed for you to come home safely, Thomas.'

He nodded and wished he could say something to her, something that would make her happy.

Just before they reached the door, Helen stopped and asked, 'Are we going to keep him?'

'Yes,' Thomas answered, 'we're going to keep him.'

The house was exactly as Thomas remembered it. Nothing was changed; not even one piece of furniture had been moved in his absence. When he entered the large front room Maria Gonzalez, the cook, came out of the kitchen to speak to Helen, took one look at him, and cried, '*Madre mia!* Thomas! Thomas! Thomas!' And she ran to him.

He embraced her warmly.

Then she stepped back and, looking at him, saw the scar on his face, and with tears in her eyes gently touched his face. 'You stay home now? No more war?'

'No more war,' he told her.

Maria looked at Helen and saw the baby in her arms.

'I found him,' Thomas explained.

Maria went closer to Helen and said, 'Negro?'

'*Él es un mulato,*' Thomas answered.

Maria cocked her head to one side and, looking at the baby, said, '*Él es muy bonito.*' She touched his face and asked, '*Cual es el nombre?*'

'Since I found him,' Thomas said. 'I've been calling him John.'

'But —' Helen started to say something, changed her mind, and said, 'Then I guess we'll call him that. You take him, Maria, for now, and see if he'll eat. I'll come to the kitchen in a little while.'

The woman took the child, and as she left for the kitchen she promised Thomas to make him a good dinner.

'With apple pie,' he called after her.

'*Sí … Sí…*' she answered.

'I want to clean up,' Thomas told Helen.

She nodded.

'For now I'll use Pa's room,' Thomas said, remembering the bad times with her.

Helen swallowed but agreed.

A short time later, after he had trimmed his beard, Thomas was soaking in the large metal bathtub. Bringing John home was much easier than he had thought it would be. But he was sure that Helen knew he had lied to her. And if she knew that, he was almost as certain that she probably guessed the boy was his own. He shrugged and scrubbed away the dirt of all the places he had been. It was good to feel clean again.

As he left the tub and wrapped a large towel around his waist. Helen knocked on the door. He knew it was her by the hesitant way she knocked. 'Come in!' he called, and faced the door.

'I brought clean duds for you,' she said, looking at him. 'But they might be a bit big on you since the last time you wore them.'

He nodded and thanked her. Helen set the clothes down on the bed and approached him. Her eyes moved over his bare shoulders and muscular arms.

Thomas gave her a nod of thanks. He wanted to dress, but felt constrained to bare his body in front of her, even though she was his wife.

Helen told him she had a few things to do and left the room.

'I'll be out shortly,' he commented.

When she reached the door Helen turned and said; 'Unless you have strong objections about it, I think you —' She stopped. 'Your place is in the master bedroom.'

'I thought you'd prefer this arrangement,' he answered.

She shrugged. 'If for no other reason,' Helen said, 'than to keep Maria's tongue from wagging.'

'I suppose that's as good as any other,' Thomas replied. He didn't consider the matter worth arguing about.

'I put John in Ethan's room,' she said.

He gave her a questioning look. He hadn't expected her to do something like that.

'The room,' she told him, 'wasn't — well, it's the only room in the house that's fit for a baby, and he's the only baby in the house, and … he's still only a baby, isn't that right?'

Thomas shrugged.

'What I do in my own house,' she said almost angrily, 'is none of anyone's business.'

'That's right,' Thomas answered.

Helen nodded and left the room.

As soon as Thomas was dressed he prowled around the house, moving from one room to another, almost as though he were looking for something. Then he went into the sitting room and found the Bible where his father always had kept it, on the shelf near the fireplace. He opened it and saw the thin black lines that ran through Clem's name and his. He heaved a deep sigh and closed the book. Then he went outside and looked around the house.

In the years he had been away it had fallen into a state of disrepair. Much of the maintenance that should have been a matter of routine couldn't be done, because most of the ranch hands were in the army and those who were left were too few and too busy trying to keep some sort of herd together.

Thomas paid a visit to the bunkhouse. Four middle-aged men stood up when he came in. One of them, a man named Luke Singein, told him that the rest of the men had long since gone off to fight.

'And what about the herd?' Thomas asked.

'Managed to keep some of it,' Luke said. 'But most is strays all over here. The injuns have been hittin' pretty hard out this way. And then there's the hired guns takin' what they please.'

'Any signs of them around here?'

The man shook his head. 'So far, Mister Carey,' Luke said, 'we've been real lucky. But not a day's ride from here three ranches were burned out.'

Thomas spoke with Luke for a few more minutes and then returned to the house. The sun had dropped low in the western sky, and the wind had more than just a hint of a chill. Thomas stood and looked at the bluish gray hills and the beginning of what was going to be a beautiful sunset.

Though he had asked about the herd, he wasn't really interested in it, at least not yet. He wanted time to let the army drain out of his system. Besides, even if he worked with the four men, there was nothing more the five of them could do than just what the four hands hadn't already done.

'Señor Thomas!' Victor Gonzalez shouted, as he came at a run around the side of the house.

Thomas went toward him, and in a quick roll of Spanish, Maria's husband told Thomas how happy he was to see him home. Then he launched into an equally rapid description of how things were at the ranch. 'And your wife,' he said, kissing the tips of his fingers, 'she's an angel, a saint … and a tower of strength. If it weren't for her, Thomas, the ranch would be gone, like so many others around Paso Diablo.'

Thomas expected Victor to place the cause of the trouble on the Indians, but to his surprise he was told that Mr Johnson was buying up the ranches.

'He's plenty bad fellow,' Gonzalez said.

'Always was,' Thomas answered, feeling the prickles race down his back. Johnson had been the middleman between Zeb and his father. His father had gone to Johnson to hire guns, and Johnson had hired Zeb. Someday Thomas hoped to meet up with the Johnson man.

'Your *padre*, he saw a lot of Johnson,' Victor said, shaking his head. 'Sometimes I think that he wanted your *padre* to sell him the ranch.' Then he smiled. 'But your *padre* don't sell. He keep it for you.'

Thomas didn't answer.

'Your wife,' Victor told him, 'she take good care of your *padre*. He very worried about his sons. You, Clem, and Juan. Most of the time he just sit in his rocking chair and go back and forth.' Victor gestured with his hand to give emphasis to what he said. 'He not able to do much.'

'You mean when he got sick,' Thomas said.

'Since you leave, Thomas,' Victor told him. 'God rest his soul, he got all mixed up in here.' And the man touched his head. 'But he love the little boy.'

Suddenly Maria began to yell for her husband.

'*Madre mia,*' Victor exclaimed, 'she still shouts too loud, don't she?'

Thomas smiled. 'You better go to her,' he said, 'or she'll come looking for you with a rolling pin in her hand.'

'You tell me about the war, Thomas?'

'Sometime, maybe.'

'*Adios*, my friend,' Victor said.

The next afternoon Thomas saddled one of the ranch's cow ponies, a sorrel named Butter, and with the dead gunman's mount in tow he rode into Paso Diablo.

The day was very hot, and to the north huge clouds were building into black mountains.

Thomas rode up the dusty main street, where a half dozen wooden structures faced each other. The courthouse, jail, and sheriff's office were in one building, and it stood at the far end of the main street. There was a small Methodist church, a livery stable, and a general store on the street. Thomas noticed the weather-beaten sign over the blacksmith's shop that said it was under new management. He wondered if Lisa and her husband lived in the loft above the shop or in the small cabin behind it.

Because of the heat there were only a few people on Main Street, and they didn't recognize Thomas. When he reached the Broken Horn Saloon he dismounted and secured the reins of both horses to the hitching post. He walked up the wooden steps and into the dimly lit bar-room. Several men were clustered at one end of the bar. None of them looked familiar to Thomas, and he chose a place some distance away from the other drinkers.

Tiny, a tall, heavy-set man, was behind the bar. He looked at the stranger and waited until Thomas had settled his elbows on the bar before asking, 'What's your pleasure?'

Thomas pushed his slouched hat back. 'Come to say hello to an old friend,' he said, hooking the heel of his right boot over the brass railing.

Tiny's eyes opened wide. 'By the living God,' he shouted, 'it's you. It's really you, Thomas!' And he thrust his beefy hand across the bar.

'You're still the same,' Thomas said, shaking Tiny's hand. 'You're still the same.'

'Hey, gents,' Tiny called, 'this is Thomas Carey. He's come back from the war. The drinks are on me. We're celebrating!'

Tiny and Thomas toasted each other's good health and fortune.

'Now tell me,' Tiny said, 'tell me what happened to you. We heard that you were missing in action. We even heard you come back for a spell about a year ago?'

Thomas shook his head.

Tiny leaned forward and, in a low voice, he said, 'Lisa waited until she heard you were missing.'

'I figured as much,' Thomas answered, downing his drink. 'I can't blame her for marrying.'

Tiny shook his head.

'Is Sheriff Wyler around?' Thomas asked.

'He's around,' Tiny said, 'but he ain't sheriff anymore.'

Thomas gave him a questioning look.

'Lots of things have changed,' Tiny told him. 'The sheriff we got now is one of Johnson's men, and so are several others. This town isn't the way it used to be. People come from up north, or renegade Southerners, have come here to pick our bones.'

Thomas saw one of the men at the end of the bar go to the door, stop, and hurriedly return to the others.

Tiny jerked his thumb toward the group at the bar and in a low voice said, 'They belong to Johnson too.'

Thomas nodded, and after finishing off another drink he said, 'I guess I'll be going. Thanks, Tiny.'

The barkeep nodded.

'Hey, Carey,' a small wiry man called, 'where you goin'? We ain't even got to know you yet.'

Thomas stopped and turned. The man was the same one who had gone to the door. 'I just come in to visit Tiny,' he said.

'With two horses?'

'No law against it,' Thomas chuckled.

The comment brought forth a chorus of rough laughter from the other men. And one said, 'Smitty, you goin' ta talk him to death before ya get ta —'

'Shut your mouth, Pike!'

'Now if you gents will excuse me,' Thomas said, 'I'll be on my way.'

'What side did you fight on?' Smitty challenged. He had moved away from the others.

Thomas shook his head. 'That's a damn fool question,' he said. 'I ain't going to be fool enough to answer it.' He clenched his fist. He knew who the man was, and he was sure that the man knew who he was.

'Hey, Smitty,' Tiny said. 'Thomas was a Confederate officer. You're wrong about him.'

'I ain't wrong about him,' Smitty snarled, 'am I, Carey?'

Thomas said nothing.

'We're goin' ta show ya,' Smitty said, 'jest what we think of people like you. All right, boys, take the bastard!'

In an instant the men were on him. He punched two down. A blow sent him crashing to the floor. A man leaped on him, but Thomas rolled away and was on his feet swinging.

'Use a rope!' someone yelled.

Several ropes whirled through the air. One caught Thomas, and in moments he was down on the floor and tied.

'All right,' Smitty said, 'we'll give him a lesson he'll never forget. Bring him outside, boys.'

They dragged Thomas into the street and tied the end of the rope to the pommel of the saddle.

'All right,' Smitty shouted as he mounted the horse, 'here we go!'

Thomas was suddenly pulled forward. He felt as if his arms were being torn from their sockets. He tried to pull himself up on the rope but couldn't. Sweat poured out of him. His face and head were battered by every rut in the street. People were watching. They were blurred, but he could see them. Some were yelling, but he could not make out what they were shouting. He tasted blood in his mouth and felt it flow from his nose. Then the roaring started in his head. The low thunder of cannon firing came from deep inside his brain and filled his skull like some dark blooming flower. And he was running down the long slope from Fort Stedman again. The earth shivered under him. Explosion after explosion followed.

Then the thunder diminished.

Thomas saw Zeb. In the night mists on the bank of the Chickahominy they fought. Thomas brought him down.

'Who sent you?'

Zeb told him.

'You lie!' Thomas shouted. 'You lie. He wouldn't do that to his own son.'

'God's own truth.'

Thomas brought his rowled spur down on Zeb's throat.

'Your pa sent me,' Zeb laughed. 'Your pa...'

Thomas tore open his throat...

Zeb's laughter drifted away even as the mists on the Chickahominy drifted away.

The light from the lamp hurt Thomas' eyes, and his head throbbed with pain. Slowly a face came close to his. It was blurred, but he knew the face. Slowly he raised his hand to it and whispered, 'Lisa?'

'*Sí*,' she answered. '*Sí*.' There was a sob in her voice.

He ran his fingers over her cheeks. They were wet with tears. 'Where am I?'

'In my old shack,' she said.

Thomas started to move. The hot rush of pain made him gasp. 'How long have I been here?' he asked, easing himself up to a sitting position.

'Since the afternoon.'

Thomas looked around. The shack was part wood and part sod. A portion of the side wall was broken, and he could see where he and Lisa had slept in each other's arms. It was no longer curtained off from the rest of the room by the Indian blanket, but the old brass bed on which he had made love to her was still there. So were the secondhand table and chairs he had bought for her. With a little patching the place would be livable again.

He took hold of Lisa's hand. Looking up at her, he asked, 'How long have you been here?'

'I come when Tiny — oh, Thomas,' she moaned softly, 'I see what they do to you an' no one will stop them. They don't stop till you start to scream 'bout cannon fire. Then Tiny, he rush out and grabs hold of the horse and pulls Smitty off…'

Thomas took a deep breath, and in an instant his head seemed to be filled with Lisa's scent. He put her hand to his lips and saw her tremble. Even filled with pain, he wanted her…

'Sleep, Thomas,' she told him, 'you'll be fine in a day or two.'

He nodded.

'I go now,' Lisa said. 'But I will be back again.' She moved away from the side of the bed. 'I know what you're thinking,' she told him in a low voice, 'but it will not happen.'

Thomas did not answer, but he moved his head and looked at her.

'It will not!' she cried definitely, and ran from the shack.

The next morning Thomas was strong enough to go down to the creek and wash. That afternoon when Tiny came to visit him, he stood at the door and said, 'Sooner or later I'm going to kill Smitty.'

'Haven't you had enough?' Tiny asked, sitting down at the crude table.

Thomas said nothing. He had already said too much.

'Just like that. Thomas, you're not the first man to get beaten up —'

'I don't give a shit about being beaten,' Thomas told him. 'There's something else —'

'Because of what he called you?'

Thomas smiled and said, 'I've been called worse.'

'If it's not them two things, then what the hell is it?'

'He and his sidekick killed a friend of mine,' Thomas said. 'When I came in with that mount I was looking for —'

Tiny's jaw went slack. 'Well, I'll be a son-of-a-bitch!' he exclaimed.

Thomas turned and looked at him.

'Smitty was right, wasn't he?'

'Maybe if you tell me what he said,' Thomas responded, 'I could tell you if he was right?'

'You were riding with a black man. That's what he said.'

Thomas left the doorway and leaned against the wall. 'I *was* riding with a black man,' he said, 'when we were bushwhacked. I killed one of them. That's how come I had his horse. Smitty is the other one. I already told you — I'm going to kill him.'

Tiny pulled out his red bandanna and wiped his sweaty brow. 'But it doesn't make any sense to get so riled up over it. Most of the men around these parts would have taken a shot at him. They're not wanted here, Thomas.'

'The war is over, Tiny…'

'But you fought to keep them in their place.'

Thomas shook his head.

'There's just no talking to you,' Tiny complained as he stepped out of the shack. 'Once you get a notion in your head, nothing but nothing changes it.'

Thomas shrugged.

'It's not just Smitty you'll be going against,' Tiny warned.

'I figured it might be a few others.'

'Johnson gets real mean when his men get killed.'

'Then he's going to be real mean for a while,' Thomas answered.

'Thomas, you're seven kinds of a fool!' Tiny gave a disdainful snort, turned away, and hurried up the path toward the Broken Horn Saloon.

NINE

It was late that night before Lisa came to the shack. When Thomas heard her footsteps on the path, he dimmed the candle and waited just inside the door.

Lisa entered the semi-darkened room and called, 'Thomas … Thomas … Thomas, where are you?'

He reached out, caught hold of her shoulder, and, spinning her around, had his lips on hers before she could cry out. For a few moments she struggled to free herself, and then he felt her strain wildly against him. He felt the heat of her lips and tasted her tongue; he felt the soft thrust of her breasts and the harder thrust of her body.

'Lisa,' he whispered passionately. 'Lisa … Lisa …' His hands fumbled with the buttons on the front of her dress, and soon his hands were on her breasts.

They separated and quickly removed their clothing.

Thomas lifted her into his arms and kissed her bare breasts. And once they were in bed each devoured the other with kisses.

'I love you,' Thomas whispered passionately, stroking her naked body and devouring its lushness with his eyes. He pressed his face to her bare breasts and kissed each erect nipple with passionate eagerness. His hands found her womanhood, and she responded by caressing him as she had so long ago in the past.

'Come,' Lisa whispered, 'come into me.' And she drew him over her, arching her body to receive his thrust.

Thomas made love to Lisa with all the passion, with all the tenderness he possessed, and Lisa gave to him the full delight of her body until they were left breathless in each other's arms.

For a long time neither of them moved but then Lisa raised her head and asked, 'And now what, Thomas?'

'You're mine,' he said, stroking her naked breast.

Lisa shook her head.

'And what does that mean?'

'I'm married to Jose Torres,' she said. 'I belong to him.'

'You're mine,' Thomas said fiercely.

'Because of this?' Lisa asked. 'Because of what we just did?' She shook her head. 'Fucking me doesn't make me yours.'

'Then why —'

'Because I am weak,' she said. 'Because I wanted to be with you again, and because it's the only thing I have to give you, Thomas.

'I don't understand,' Thomas told her.

She took hold of his hand and put it on her bare stomach. 'I carry his child.'

Thomas pulled his hand away. 'You should have waited for me, Lisa. You should have waited.'

'I did,' she answered. 'Then Tiny said you were not to be found.'

'Missing.'

'Missing,' Lisa repeated.

'I was captured by the Yankees,' he explained. 'But I escaped.'

'No one told me —'

'No one knew,' he said. 'But now —'

Lisa shook her head. 'Jose gave me his name and a home of my own,' she told him softly. 'He took me for his wife, even though I was a saloon girl. He is a good man, Thomas, a very good man.'

'But you don't love him,' Thomas said. 'I know you don't love him.'

'I do,' she told him quietly. 'I love him for being good to me, for never telling me I was a whore.'

Her words made him cringe.

'Thomas, you have a wife and I have a husband,' Lisa said. 'I have never forgotten you,' she said. 'I have always prayed for you.'

'It's not your prayers I want,' Thomas said hotly. 'It's you.' And he tried to embrace her again.

'No!' she exclaimed, moving away.

Thomas dropped his hand and glared at her.

'Your anger will pass,' she told him in a low voice.

He said nothing.

There was a buckboard in the front yard when Thomas rode in. It belonged to his father-in-law, Sam Wicker, a tall, sparse man who had owned more slaves than anyone else around Paso Diablo before the war, and who believed in the Confederacy as he believed in the Holy Writ.

There was damn little that either of them could say or do that would not make the other angrier than an old mossback on the end of a rope. Thomas swung out of the saddle, slipped the reins around the hitching post, and entered the house.

Sam turned around. He was standing in front of the big hearth, and when he saw his son-in-law his face went white with anger.

Thomas nodded to him and looked at Helen. She was standing to the right of her father, and John was in her arms. Thomas took off his hat and jacket and put both of them on pegs behind the door. Then he removed his gun belt and looped it over another peg. No one said anything, but as Thomas walked to the table the wooden floor creaked loudly.

'Pa told me you were in a fight,' Helen finally said. Her voice was weary and flat.

'I told her to come home and leave the baby with you,' Sam said, 'seeing as how you're so all fired up to have him.'

'Things haven't changed much,' Thomas commented with a sigh.

'I would have thought,' Sam told him, '*you* had done some changing. Like I told Helen, you'll never be any good!' he exclaimed, almost shrilly.

'Sam,' Thomas said quietly, 'I don't want to have any hard words with you, at least not the first time I see you.'

'Helen,' her father asked, 'are you going to raise this child?'

Thomas' hand jumped out. He grabbed hold of the man by his jacket. 'The boy's name is John,' he said harshly. Then, looking straight at Helen, he added, 'John Carey.' He let go of Sam and, in a softer voice, said, 'His mother saved my life.' He went to Helen and took the child from her. 'She was a fine woman.' And then his voice became hard again. 'Don't ever, Sam, call my son by anything but his name.'

'You coming with me, Helen?' Sam asked.

'You go, Pa,' she said softly.

'What —'

'Go, Pa,' she said resolutely. 'I'll come to see you by and by.'

Sam stomped out of the house and slammed the door behind him.

'He's right,' Thomas told her after he heard Sam's buggy leave the yard.

'I know,' Helen answered, and she took the child from him. Looking at the baby, she said, 'I knew he was your son from the moment I laid eyes on him.' She lifted her face to Thomas. 'I'm past anger,' she told him, 'and long past being hurt. I'll do for him as I would have done for my own, had the good Lord seen fit to let him live.'

Thomas nodded.

'But it's not me alone,' she said, 'who has to do for him.'

He looked at her questioningly.

'Since you've given him your name,' Helen said, 'you're beholden to give him everything that goes with it. And that means the ranch, when the time comes.'

'I know that,' he answered. He did not know what she was getting at, but whatever it was, she was sure taking her time.

'I own it, Thomas,' Helen told him.

He swallowed and, in a whisper, asked, 'The ranch?'

Helen nodded. 'Your daddy left it to me.'

Thomas was speechless.

'He said to give it back to you when you've earned it.'

The old anger against his father filled Thomas. 'He always managed to beat me,' he said tightly. 'Always. But why didn't you tell me when I was home —'

'It wouldn't have mattered then,' Helen answered. 'But now the war is over and you're home.'

'I never believed he would do it,' Thomas said, shaking his head. 'I put my sweat into this place —'

'It needs more of it,' Helen told him. Her voice was hard.

'Tell me straight out — what's on your mind?'

'Unless you get this ranch going,' she said, 'I'll sell it.'

'You'd do something like that?'

She nodded.

He turned his back to her.

'There are thousands of head out there,' she said. 'And the North is hungry for Texas beef.'

Thomas faced her again and asked, 'Is that the deal?'

'If you want the ranch back,' she told him, 'I don't see that you have much choice but to take it.'

'You've backed me against the wall, Helen.'

She shrugged and said, 'Not me, Thomas. Not me. I was never strong enough to do that. But your son, small as he is, is stronger than I ever was.'

Thomas stared at the wall. Nothing he could say would change matters.

'Do you want me to sell?'

'No!' he exclaimed angrily. 'No.' And in a softer voice, he said, 'I'll do what you want.'

For the next few days Thomas rode the range. From sunup to sundown he looked for and found critters. Helen was absolutely right: There were thousands of them within twenty to thirty miles of the ranch. Some were at least six-year-old mossbacks, and all were landinos, never having been branded and possibly never having seen a rider. They bunched together in the brush or in coulees and draws.

But to do anything with them they would have to be flushed out of their hiding places, branded, herded, and then trailed to a railhead in the North, some place like Caldwell or Kansas City. Either of those places was a good way away, maybe a thousand miles or more. That kind of drive was best started in the spring, not late summer. But a small herd might make it up north before winter set in. It was something to think about. And the more time Thomas spent in the saddle, the more he did think about it. But at night, when he returned to the ranch he said nothing to Helen about the plan that was taking shape in his mind.

That his father had given her the ranch cut Thomas deeply, forcing all the old memories to come out of their dark corners. He had married Helen to hold on to the ranch. His father said one went with the other. And when William said something, he meant it.

Not a day passed without Thomas also seeing evidence of Indians. A few abandoned camp sites were Apache; others were Kiowa. Half a day's ride from the ranch he came across the remains of a slaughter in what had been an Apache camp with women and children. He followed the trail north for a while, but saw no sign of them and turned back.

Hours later, when darkness lay over the land and the sky was filled with chips of starlight, Thomas rode into the front yard. Though he was tired, Thomas felt good. He had firmed up in his mind what he was going to do, and decided that it was time to tell Helen. After stabling his mount he walked back to the house. The window was filled with a yellow light.

He stopped. The house was too quiet. Familiar sounds were missing. Prickles rose on his back. His throat went dry and he licked his lips. Off in the distance a coyote barked and was quickly answered.

Suddenly the front door opened. In the half-light he saw Helen. It was unlike her to come out and greet him. Usually she waited until after he had washed and was already seated at the table before she would speak to him.

'Thomas,' Helen said, 'I've been waiting for you.'

He was sure now that something was wrong. He softly cleared his throat and answered, 'I rode all the way to Twin Rocks.' He lengthened his steps but did not quicken his stride.

'That's a lot of ridin',' a man said, 'fer nothin'.' He spoke at almost the same time he stepped behind Helen.

Thomas' hand dropped, but stopped before it ever reached the handle of his gun. There was no way he could fire without hitting Helen. His breath became caught in his throat, forcing him to cough several times.

'Best come inside, Mister Carey,' the man said. 'I ain't too partial to night air.' The man moved back and gently eased Helen off to one side, out of the doorway. 'Don't go for your gun, Mister Carey. I wouldn't want to have one of my men kill you in your own house, especially when I come to talk to you.'

Thomas raised his hands and entered the house. The man who spoke to him was lean and cadaverous-looking, with deep, sunken brown eyes.

He waved Thomas toward the table and said, 'Let's sit.' And to the two men who stood near the window with their guns drawn he said, 'Why don't you boys bring the mounts out front and wait for me.'

The men hesitated.

'Don't worry none,' he assured them. 'Mister Carey and me have some business to talk about.'

The gunmen holstered their Colts and left the house.'

'You can lower your hands, Mister Carey. My name is Pete Wheeler.' And he offered Thomas his hand.

'Hard to shake the hand of a man,' Thomas told him, 'who comes to your house and holds a gun on you.'

Wheeler shrugged, a pinpoint of light blazing deep in his eyes, and said with a laugh, 'At least you don't waste words, Carey.'

'I don't waste much of anything.'

'Now that's where you're wrong,' Wheeler said. 'You're dead wrong there, Carey. All this ridin' out on the range you're doin' is not only a waste of time but of strength too. Those cows out there won't ever do you any good.'

'Is that a fact?' Thomas asked, sitting down at the table. Wheeler sat down opposite him and said, 'Suppose I tell you that a certain party is willin' to buy you out?'

Thomas chuckled. He glanced knowingly at Helen, who was standing in front of the closed door to John's room. And then he shifted his gaze to Wheeler. 'Tell Mister Johnson that Thomas Carey isn't selling. Teil him that he claims all the critters with his brand —'

'But none of them cows have ever been branded, at least not in the past few years.'

'I'm going to change that,' Thomas said.

Wheeler leaned back and rubbed his clean-shaven chin. 'Right here and now,' he said. 'I can offer you twenty thousand in gold for this place, and from the shape it's in I'd say that was a mighty good price.'

Thomas shook his head, and again glanced at Helen. Except for the tightness around the corners of her mouth, her face was expressionless.

'Twenty-five.'

'I'm not selling,' Thomas said.

'Thirty. And that's as high as —'

'I'm going to put the WC brand on everything that has four legs and horns,' Thomas said. 'Tell Johnson that. Tell him —' He almost said something about having a score to settle with him, but instead he muttered, 'Those are my final words. Now, if you'll excuse me, I'm about to eat my dinner.'

'Forty thousand in gold!' Wheeler offered.

'Helen,' Thomas said, 'would you tell Maria to serve dinner.'

Wheeler made a motion with his hand that stopped Helen from moving, and he said, 'Now, Missus Carey, maybe you can talk some sense to your husband.'

'She has nothing to do with it!' Thomas exclaimed hotly.

Wheeler looked at him. 'She mightn't want to be a widow woman,' he said. 'Mister Johnson can get mighty touchy about things, especially about something like his cows.'

'They're not his yet. They're there for the taking,' Thomas said. 'And several thousand head come from his ranch.'

Wheeler shook his head. 'You're a fool,' he told him, 'if you think you can —'

'I can,' Thomas said, 'and I sure as hell will.'

'You're makin' trouble for you and yours.'

Helen gasped.

Wheeler looked at her, but spoke to Thomas. 'Meanin' no disrespect to your wife, Carey, but it seems to me that you've already given her enough trouble. Don't bring any more. And now I hear tell you got yourself a baby. Be right shameful if that child lost his pa and ma. There's no one hereabout who would care for him.'

Thomas clenched his teeth in hate.

'I'm just tellin' you the plain truth, Carey,' Wheeler said. 'Now if you took Mister Johnson's offer of forty — I'll make it fifty — fifty thousand in gold, you could go north and really live the life…'

Thomas said nothing. But even as Wheeler was telling him how he wouldn't have any trouble, Thomas eased his right hand down below the level of the table. In a low flat voice he said, 'Wheeler, it's time for you to leave.'

The man gave him a questioning look. But in the next instant he realized what had happened. 'I have two men outside,' he said, challengingly.

'You said what you came to say,' Thomas told him. 'Now ride.'

'Don't come cryin' when things get rough. You had your chance. Don't complain that Mister Johnson didn't give you a chance.'

Thomas nodded.

'You won't get anyone to ride for you,' Wheeler told him.

'Let me worry about that. Now you just stand up. Slow, Wheeler, or you're a dead man. Walk very slow to the door.' Thomas swung around, covering the man with the Colt. By the time Wheeler reached the door, Thomas was behind him. 'That's right. Now tell your boys to mount up.'

Wheeler did what he was told to do.

'Now go,' Thomas said.

'You're a fool,' Wheeler called from the saddle, 'a damn fool!'

'Ride,' Thomas shouted at the trio, 'or I'll kill every mother's son of you … Ride!'

The three men pounded out of the front yard and up the trail that led to Paso Diablo.

Thomas walked outside, going as far as the fence. He waited there for some time to make sure that Wheeler and his sidekicks had not swung around once they were out of sight. When he was satisfied that they were not coming back, at least not right away, he returned to the house.

While he was gone, Helen had put dinner on the table. Thomas sat down. Suddenly he felt very tired.

He looked at the roasted chicken and, shaking his head, told Helen that he had lost his appetite. 'That Wheeler feller,' he said, 'took the edge off it. The only thing I want to do is soak in a hot tub and maybe sleep for a couple or three years.'

'Do you think he means —'

'He means it,' Thomas said.

'Then there'll be killing?' she asked.

'Most likely,' he answered with a nod.

Helen heaved a deep sigh.

'You're not figuring on selling, are you?'

'No,' she said softly. 'But I wish there was some other way of —'

With a wave of his hand, Thomas silenced her. He did not want to hear what she wished for, since it had nothing whatsoever to do with the way things were. And he would have said as much to her if she had gone on palavering, but she kept quiet.

Thomas rolled a cigarette and after taking several drags on it he said in a low voice, 'There's more between me and Johnson than cows.'

'I don't understand,' she said.

Thomas stood up, went to the cabinet on the far side of the room, and, opening one of the doors, took down a bottle of whiskey. He brought it back to the table and poured himself a tumbler full. He took a long swallow, and before the warmth flooded his being he finished all that was in the glass and poured himself another generous amount.

'Are you going to sit here and drink?' Helen asked.

'That looks pretty much like what I'm doing,' he answered, gesturing to her with the tumbler.

'Why —'

'No questions, Helen,' he said. 'No questions, not now. Now I just want you to listen to me. When I came home the last time I came to kill —'

'No, don't,' she cried. 'I don't want to hear about it.'

'My pa,' he told her, 'went to Johnson —' Helen leaped to her feet. But Thomas grabbed hold of her wrist and, forcing her to sit down again, he said, 'My pa went to Johnson, and Johnson hired Zeb —'

'Oh God, Thomas,' Helen gasped, 'why are you doing this?'

'Because,' he answered gruffly, 'because it sticks in my craw.' He nodded and, squinting at her, he said, 'Zeb came after me and killed several good men to get at me. But in the end I killed him … I killed him … I tore his throat open with my spur. I tore his throat open, Helen…'

She was silently weeping. He let go of her.

'I never knew,' she told him. 'I swear to you, Thomas, I never knew.'

Thomas repeated her words, nodded and, moving his hand, he accidentally knocked the tumbler to the floor. Miraculously, it did not shatter. Thomas looked down at it, smiled, and set his head down on the table. In a matter of moments he was asleep.

TEN

Putting a herd together under a blazing August sun for branding with only four hands was slow, hard work. Each morning Thomas and the other men would be in the saddle and riding before the rim of the range to the east bled red.

All of them flushed cows from the brush and ran them out of the coulees and draws. Wherever a rider combed for cows, clouds of yellow dust bloomed. Two of the hands bunched and moved the stock to the holding place. When night came every man pulled his tour of riding guard around the herd.

When there were twelve hundred head in the herd, Thomas began working them.

Groups of twenty were cut out of the bawling, bellowing bunch of cows, and one by one each animal was roped, thrown, and branded WC. The stink of singed hair and burnt flesh hung heavy in the air. But by the end of a week the work was finished. Thomas held half of the cows he branded for the trail and turned the other half loose.

'Not a bad showing,' Luke said as they looked over the herd of six hundred head.

'It won't mean a damn unless we can sell them,' Thomas answered.

'Selling them won't be hard,' Luke commented, 'but gettin' to where we can sell them, that's goin' ta be a real chop buster.' He jabbed his thumb to the southwest. 'We've had company for most of the day.'

'I've seen them,' Thomas told the man. 'But as long as they stay where they are and we're here, well, the range is big enough for us and whoever they are.' He pulled the wide brim of his sombrero low over his eyes. 'If we don't get some rain soon,' he commented, 'this range is going to start to blow away.'

'That's for sure,' Luke answered.

Thomas told him that he wanted at least one man to stay with the herd all the time. 'I don't want to have to look for strays before moving them out.'

Luke touched his forefinger to the rim of his hat. Then he said, 'Me and the others watched you, Mister Carey —' He stopped for a moment. 'See, we know you got your ways an' other folks hereabouts might not care for them. But we want you to know that it don't matter none with us.'

Thomas nodded and, swinging his mount around, headed back to the ranch. Later at dinner he told Helen that he would begin driving the herd north on the following Monday.

'To where?' she asked.

'If I can get a couple more riders and a wrangler, I might try to go up to Kansas City.'

'How long will you be gone?'

'Maybe, if I'm lucky,' he answered, with a shrug, 'I'll be back early in November.'

Thomas left the table and went into John's room. The child was asleep. He looked at the boy for several moments. Since John had come to the ranch he had grown, or at least it seemed so to Thomas. The child definitely had some of his mother's features, especially her high cheekbones. Jenny had had some Cherokee blood in her. Thomas gently touched the boy's face.

'You'll wake him,' Helen said.

He turned. Helen was standing in the doorway, watching him.

'You know,' she commented, 'you go in to look at him every night after dinner.'

Thomas shrugged and walked out of the room, closing the door after him. 'I can't imagine myself ever being so small,' he told her. 'I look at him and I think of all the things that will happen to him by the time he gets to be my size.'

'I know what you mean,' she answered. 'Sometimes it seems to me that just the other day I was a young woman without a care in the world, and now —' She stopped.

Thomas flushed.

'I didn't mean it the way it sounded,' Helen quickly explained. 'What I really meant to say was that so many things happen to us that we can't even begin to guess what they will be.'

'I reckon that's so,' Thomas answered. He went to the front door, opened it, and looked up at the night sky. 'Maybe if we knew,' he said more to himself than to her, 'we might never want to go the full trail.'

'I don't believe that,' she responded, coming alongside him. 'At least not about you.'

Thomas felt her presence, and it made him uneasy.

'After Zeb and the other two finished with me,' Helen said quietly, 'I wanted to die, I really did…'

Thomas became more uneasy. There was something different about her. He glanced at her, trying to catch a glimpse of what it might be.

'I can't imagine you,' she told him, 'ever feeling that way.'

'I have,' he said simply.

'I wouldn't have thought so,' she commented after a pause.

He chuckled and said, 'You know only the good die young.'

'Oh, get on with you, Thomas!' she exclaimed.

There was an unmistakable lilt in her voice, girlish enough to make him look at her. She was half turned toward him. Even in the darkness her long hair looked like corn silk. Her lips were slightly parted. She seemed to be trying to speak but unable to get the words out of her throat. She raised her hand and touched his face.

He shook his head and whispered, 'Let things be, Helen.'

'I can't,' she told him.

He took hold of her hand and gently lowered it. 'I love you,' she said softly.

He shook his head and told her, 'It's just not enough for me to have a loving wife during the day.'

'You mean out of bed, don't you?'

Her frankness surprised him, but he quickly recovered and answered, 'I'm a man of flesh and blood.'

Helen nodded, and in a whisper said, 'Do you know how many nights since you've been home I've longed for you —' She stopped. 'I know how I must look to you, but the rest of me is undamaged. I've come to understand, Thomas, that I'm also made of flesh and blood —' She turned away and stifled her sobs. 'I once told you,' she continued without looking at him, 'that I would make you love me, and to prove it I gave myself to you. But I was wrong then: I couldn't make you love me, but Thomas, I have loved you. I still love you, and I will always love you …'

She faced him again. Thomas sighed. Sooner or later, something like this had to happen. A man and a woman could not continue to sleep in the same bed and never do with each other what nature had intended them to. But all her past refusals had stopped him from ever reaching out for her.

'Each night,' Helen told him, 'I've hoped that…' Her voice faltered. 'I hoped that you'd come to me.'

'Don't, Helen,' he said, knowing how much it must be hurting her pride to say what she was saying. 'There's no need.'

'But there is a need!' she exclaimed with vehemence. 'There's *my* need, Thomas. I'm still a young woman … I'm not old, Thomas!'

He closed his eyes. The insides of his lids were green, and flecks of white zigzagged across them like specks of dust in a shaft of sunlight. When he opened them Helen was no longer standing in the doorway. He heard her run through the house to the bedroom. He went after her.

'Leave me be,' Helen wept, flinging herself down on the bed.

Thomas sat down next to her. He put his hand on her shoulder and said, 'I'm not worth all this fuss, Helen. I've brought you, like Mister Wheeler said, nothing but trouble from the very beginning.'

Helen sat up. 'It's Lisa, isn't it? You still love her, don't you?'

He was silent.

'I could even stand that,' she told him, 'if there were times when — when I had you too.' And, sobbing, she flung herself into his arms. 'I'm begging you, Thomas, I'm begging you…'

He stroked her head.

'I'm not asking that you love me, Thomas,' she wept. 'I know you don't. A long time ago I thought my love would be enough … but, dear God, it is not … it is not … I want to feel something again, Thomas. I'm hollow, all hollow inside…'

He set her down on the bed, and, brushing the tears from her cheeks, he said, 'I never wanted to hurt you, Helen.'

'I know that,' she answered with a nod.

Thomas reached down and began opening the buttons on her dress.

Helen closed her eyes and sighed deeply…

For a Saturday night the Broken Horn was practically deserted. There were a few men seated at tables along the sides, and a few more standing at the bar. Several of the women, for lack of customers, were idling their time away by the open door, where it was somewhat cooler.

Thomas was at the bar drinking and talking to Tiny, whenever the barkeep drifted down to his end of the bar. But for the most part Thomas was busy looking over the men in the bar, trying to decide which few he would speak to about working for him. All of them were strangers, and seemed to be either too young or too old for the demands of a trail drive.

He poured another drink, downed it, and let his thoughts stray to Helen. The passion with which she had met his embraces had surprised and pleased him — and, from what he could see, also surprised and pleased her. He smiled to himself.

'You look like the cat that got the mouse,' Tiny said, coming back to where Thomas was standing.

'Well, to tell the truth,' he said, 'I feel that way.'

Tiny nodded. 'Yeah,' he said, 'sometimes I feel that way too. But not tonight.' He gestured out toward the room. 'It's a slow night. It's been slow for too damn many nights.' He pulled the rag off his left shoulder and with it he began to vigorously rub the top of the bar, bringing it to a high gloss.

Thomas nodded sympathetically.

'I hear you put yourself together a herd,' Tiny said, putting the rag back on his shoulder.

'That's right.'

'Put your brand on them?'

'Ever hear of a rancher not branding his cows?'

'Now what are you going to do with them?'

'Drive them north.'

Tiny snorted.

'I'll bet you ten dollars even,' Thomas said, 'that I'll bring those critters to a market.'

'I'll take it,' Tiny said, reaching across the bar to shake Thomas' hand. 'If the Indians don't turn you back, there'll be others who will.'

'Willing to go another ten?' Thomas asked.

'Sure,' Tiny said, and then with a laugh said, 'I think my pappy used to say, "A sucker and his gold is soon parted." Speaking of gold, have you ever heard anything about the gold taken out of Richmond before the Yankees got the city?'

Thomas nodded.

'Think there's anything to it?'

'Might be,' Thomas answered with a shrug.

'Some fellers were in here this afternoon, talking.

They seemed sure that it's come west and is in these parts.'

'More than likely,' Thomas commented, 'the story has come here but the gold is somewhere else.'

'This one feller seemed mighty certain it was here,' Tiny said. 'He talked like he really knew.'

'Everyone I've ever heard spoke that way.'

'But suppose there is all that gold?'

'Then you can be damn sure it isn't just moving around on its own,' Thomas said.

'You trying to tell me,' Tiny chuckled, 'those who have it won't be eager to share —'

'I'd say they would be more than willing to fight.'

'So would I,' Tiny said with a nod.

Thomas poured himself another drink. 'You wouldn't know which of the men might be looking to hire on —'

'For your drive?'

'I need a wrangler, a cook, and an extra trail hand or two.'

'Even if there were some men here, I doubt if they'd ride for you.'

'Wheeler?'

'Him, and the fact that most men don't hold with you for what you did.'

Thomas turned and swept the room with his eyes. There was no way for him to know which of the men —

The door suddenly swung open and a tall, wiry-built young man entered.

'That's Simon,' Tiny said from behind Thomas.

'Lisa's brother?'

'The very same. He sort of grew up while you were away, didn't he? He's been riding for Darby.'

'Even carries a gun,' Thomas commented, noticing the Walker Colt on his right hip.

'Good with it too, from what I hear.'

Simon stepped up to the bar, pushed his slouch hat back, and was about to order a drink when Thomas said, 'Have one on me, Simon.'

The young man moved his head sideways.

For a moment there was a questioning look in the young man's black eyes, and then one of surprise. 'Thomas?' he asked hesitantly. 'Thomas Carey?'

Thomas smiled and nodded. Simon had been like a kid brother to Thomas.

An instant later Simon was greeting him Mexican-style and pounding Thomas on his shoulder. 'I didn't know you were home. If I'd known, I'd-a rode out to see you.'

'Didn't Lisa —'

Simon moved away and faced the bar. 'I don't have anything to do with her anymore,' he said.

'Oh!'

'She went her way and I went mine.'

'It sometimes happens that way between kin,' Thomas said.

Simon nodded and asked if Thomas' offer for a drink was still good.

'Sure it is.'

'I'll have the same as you,' Simon said.

Tiny set a glass down for the young man. Thomas poured a drink for Simon and one for himself.

'Here's to you, Thomas,' Simon toasted.

'To both of us —'

'Hey thar, Simon,' a man called from the doorway, 'you shouldn't be drinkin' with the likes of him.'

Thomas looked into the mirror behind the bar. Smitty was just inside the saloon. Two of his buddies flanked him.

'I done beat him up jest a few days back, an' now he's come fer more,' Smitty laughed.

The men at the bar moved to the sides of the room.

'Don't pay him any mind,' Thomas said in a low voice. 'We won't give him a fight until he comes right out and begs for it.'

Simon nodded and took half his whiskey down.

'Hey, Simon,' Smitty pressed, 'ain't ya heard me?'

'I drink with a friend,' he answered.

'Whose friend?' Smitty asked. 'Yours or your sister's?'

'My friend,' Simon said hotly.

'I'd be your friend too,' Smitty taunted, 'if you fixed it so I could fuck your sister.'

Simon moved. His gun cleared leather —

A flame flicked out of Smitty's gun. A sharp crack followed.

Simon screamed and was jerked backward.

Another spit of flame. Another sharp crack, and a second slug tore into Simon, flinging him across the bar.

Thomas dropped to the floor and squeezed off three shots. The first took the side of Smitty's face off. The other two slammed the man on each side of him to the door. He fired a fourth time and drove Smitty out of the door into the street.

Moments after the shooting stopped, the women were screaming and the men were running into the street yelling about the gunfight.

Thomas leaped to his feet, and with his gun still smoking he lifted Simon in his arms.

'Someone get the doc, for the love of God — get the doc!' he shouted.

'Had to do it,' Simon wheezed. 'Had to … People always said things about you an' Lisa, always…' Blood started to run from his mouth.

'Don't talk,' Thomas said, cradling the young man in his arms. He stretched him on top of the bar.

'Lisa,' he said, 'is my sister…' His eyes opened wide and, looking at Thomas, he cried out, 'I'm afraid, Thomas … I'm afraid to die!'

Then his head fell loosely to one side.

'Simon?' Thomas shouted. 'Simon?'

'It's no use,' Tiny said, looking down at the boy, 'he's dead.'

Thomas shook his head. He holstered his gun and started to lift Simon's body.

'Let me help,' Tiny offered.

'No,' Thomas said in a choked voice, 'I have to carry this burden alone.'

'Lisa is here,' Tiny said softly.

Holding Simon in his arms, Thomas turned. Lisa stopped. Thomas walked slowly toward her.

She took a step back and looked as if she wanted to run. Then she whispered, 'How, Thomas? How was my brother killed?'

Thomas shook his head. Tears spilled down his weather-beaten cheeks. He tried to speak, but could not get the knot out of his throat.

Lisa took a step forward now and blocked Thomas' way. 'Simon,' she called gently. 'Simon?' Her eyes went to Thomas' face. 'You let him die,' she said. 'You let him —'

'I didn't want him to fight,' he said brokenly. 'I didn't want—'

'He wanted to be like you,' Lisa told him. 'Even when he was a little boy he wanted to be like you, Thomas. He carried a gun like you, Thomas, and he learn to use it like you. I tell him it's no good. It's no good. But he tell me it's good. It's good because he's like you, Thomas. He's like you…'

'I couldn't stop him,' Thomas explained. 'I — there wasn't time.'

"There's never time,' Lisa answered. "Never time…' She reached over and closed her brother's eyes. Then she shouted. 'I hate you, Thomas … I hate you, Thomas Carey!' And, gathering a wad of saliva in her mouth, she spat into Thomas' face.

Thomas' head jerked back, but he said nothing.

Lisa tore the body from his arms. Faltering under its weight, she made her way slowly out of the Broken Horn.

'Thomas,' Tiny called from behind the bar.

He turned.

'She didn't mean —'

Thomas waved him silent. He followed Lisa out of the saloon. Moments later he called to her, but she never slowed her step or looked back.

ELEVEN

A day before the drive got under way, Luke hired three new men. Dandy and Bunt were signed on as drovers, and Stretch as the wrangler. The three were young men straight from the war. If they knew anything about what took place in the Broken Horn, they didn't say, and Luke didn't ask.

For the first few days of the drive Thomas pushed the herd very hard in order to move them away from familiar range and trailbreak them as quickly as possible.

It was work that began when the range was still shrouded in darkness, and lasted until just before the last light left the western sky. And then every man, with the exception of Victor, who was cook, did his stint of night herding.

During the day Thomas rode lead, while Luke, his segundo, was swing. Dandy took the flank opposite Luke, and Bunt followed in drag, bellowing and quirting at those cows that needed hurrying along. Stretch headed the remuda of thirty mounts. Though short-handed, they managed to move the herd some forty miles.

But this day seemed to be hotter than the previous four, and Thomas decided to throw the herd off the trail as soon as they came to a decent bed. He wiped the grit out of the corners of his eyes and spurred his mount into an easy lope.

About a mile in front of the herd Thomas found a piece of flat ground with enough bluestem on it to graze a herd three times the size of the one he was trailing. He reined in and, waving his hat around his head, signaled the hands to begin moving the cows toward him. Then he set the hat back on his head, pulled down the brim, and took time to roll a cigarette.

Once Thomas was smoking, he squinted at the sun. It was a yellow ball hanging low in the sky. On either side of it were red feather-like clouds. But to the north the clouds changed. They were darker, much darker, and building very high…

As he sat there waiting for the herd to come up, Thomas searched every quadrant of the compass. So far they had seen no other riders, though the day before they had spotted Indian smoke. But it was too far away for Luke to read.

When Thomas was satisfied that they were not being trailed, he lowered his line of sight and tried not to think of Simon's death. He was bothered by it as much as he ever was by anything else. There was no reason for the boy to die, and yet

—

The bawling of the herd cut his thoughts. He waved Luke on to join him. 'I figured,' Thomas explained when his segundo came alongside, 'that we could all stand a rest.'

'I sure can,' Luke responded and then, pointing to a brown critter, said, 'That old twist-horn has taken the lead. He's a big bastard, ain't he?'

'Sure is,' Thomas acknowledged. 'He had to be busted to be branded.'

'Doesn't seem to have hurt him none.'

'Hell, no!'

The herd was up now, and everyone took part in riding them down. Bunt urged the drag toward the point, and Luke swung the point to meet the drag.

'Give them enough room,' Luke shouted above the noise of the milling cows. 'Don't pack them too tightly … Give 'em room…'

Thomas turned away from the herd and went toward the chuck wagon. Victor was already at work fixing dinner, and some distance away Stretch was rope-corralling his remuda for the night. He looked back at the herd. The big brown twist-horn, and several other cows, were already down. Now that the herd had a leader, they would be easier to handle.

Thomas nodded with satisfaction, and was just about to swing out of the saddle when he saw a puff of dust bloom to the southwest. He watched it for a few moments. When he was sure it was coming toward the herd, he turned his mount and raced back to where Luke was. 'Over there,' Thomas called out, even before he reached the man.

Luke stood up. The other men also looked toward the oncoming riders.

'Don't seem like injuns,' Luke said. 'But best let's have a look at them.'

'Stay with the herd,' Thomas ordered him. 'Stretch, you come with me.' Without giving Luke a chance to say anything, he galloped toward the dust puff. Some distance from the herd, Thomas slowed to a canter. Stretch came alongside, and the two continued without speaking.

When they were close enough to see several riders under the cloud of yellow dust, Thomas said, 'They're not Indians.'

'Might be better if'n they wuz,' Stretch commented.

Thomas threw him a questioning look. But since the man made no effort to explain, Thomas was not going to press it.

There were four riders coming toward them. They were moving at a good pace, and Thomas told Stretch, 'We might as well hold here.'

'Might as well,' Stretch answered.

The four riders slowed down, and about a hundred yards away from Thomas they brought their mounts to a walk.

Because the late-afternoon sun was behind them and to their left, Thomas could not see their faces. As he fixed his eyes on their bodies, his right hand hung above his gun.

The riders stopped and one of them yelled out, 'Who are you?'

Thomas was reluctant to shout his name to a stranger. But rather than start a ruckus, he yelled, 'Thomas Carey of the WC —'

'Well, I'll be damned!' the other man shouted. 'Say, friend, don't you remember me?'

Thomas looked at Stretch and, with a shrug, said, 'How the hell can I remember him if I can't see him?'

'McTavish,' the man bellowed. 'Bud McTavish!'

Thomas let out a yell and spurred his mount forward. In moments he was shaking the hand of the chunky, barrel-chested Scotsman.

'One of my boys told me that some crazy man is trailin' a herd north,' McTavish said with rich laughter, 'and I jest figured to come out an' see for myself the man with balls big enough to do it.'

'You're looking at him,' Thomas said.

'Might have known it was you,' McTavish said. 'Your daddy must be right proud.'

'He's dead.'

McTavish clicked his tongue sympathetically.

'And your son, Billy,' Thomas asked, remembering the boy's name. 'Did he ever make it home?'

'No,' the man answered softly. 'He's still counted as missin'.'

'I'm sorry,' Thomas said, and he quickly asked about Mrs McTavish.

'Holdin' up,' McTavish answered. 'Holdin' up. But why don't you ride over an' see her? I know she'd be happy to see you again, especially since one of my men has told her he remembers a boy like Billy in the Yankee prison he was in before he busted out.'

Thomas felt the prickles rise on his back. He declined the invitation with a shake of his head, but suggested that McTavish and his men take supper with him at the chuck wagon. 'It won't be the same as your wife's cooking,' Thomas apologized, 'but Victor is a damn sight better than most trail cooks.'

'It's fine with me,' McTavish said. 'Besides, it'll give me a chance to talk business with you.'

By the time they reached the chuck wagon, Bunt was fathering the herd and Luke was pacing up and down along the side of the wagon like an expectant father. Thomas introduced McTavish and his hands to Luke and Dandy. And by the time twilight had set in, Victor had prepared one of his specialties, Sonofabitch Stew.

Thomas, though extremely curious about the man who had spent time in a Yankee prison, could think of no way of asking about him without showing his curiosity. If the man had been one of those who had sworn to kill him, there would be another gunfight. And if something happened to him, what would happen to —

'Thomas,' the Scotsman said, 'I often wondered if you got to take care of whatever it was that brought you back from the war?'

'It was taken care of,' Thomas answered, 'before I got home.'

McTavish nodded, waited a few moments, and said, 'We've been having our problems here between the Indians and Johnson's guns. Have you run into his man Wheeler yet?'

'I have,' Thomas answered.

'Imagine a mother lovin' somethin' like that?' McTavish asked with a laugh.

'Takes a powerful lot of imagining,' Thomas responded.

'Too bad we couldn't have a drink on that,' the man said.

As soon as Dandy was finished eating, he left the group to relieve Stretch and take his stint at night herding. McTavish complimented Victor on his cooking and then suggested that he and Thomas 'walk a spell'. Thomas nodded and joined McTavish in a short stroll around the chuck wagon.

'I want to throw in with you,' McTavish said.

Thomas was about to object.

'Hear me out,' the man said.

'I'm listening,' Thomas told him.

'I'll give a thousand head. Take them north, and I'll split whatever you get for them.'

'With the men I have —'

'I'll give you three, no, four of my boys, and their pay comes out of my cut. The way I see it,' McTavish said, 'I can't lose what I don't have … I've got to gamble that you'll get through.'

Thomas nodded. He understood exactly what McTavish meant. He was taking exactly the same gamble.

'Then it's a deal,' Thomas answered, shaking on it. 'But there's something I think you should know.'

'All right,' McTavish said with a nod, 'tell me.'

Thomas turned toward the chuck wagon. The men clustered around the fire were silhouetted by its wavering light. He prodded the sun-dried grass with the toe of his right boot. 'I was in a Yankee prison,' he said.

'I should think,' McTavish chuckled, 'that was the fate of a good many —'

'I might have been in the same one as your son.'

'But you told us that you never ran into Billy.'

'That's right,' Thomas said. 'But I didn't know all of the men by name.'

'Then I don't understand —'

Thomas told him how he had escaped from the column of prisoners. Then he said, 'I knew that I might be able to make it on my own, but I wasn't sure that it could be done with —'

'You left all of those men?'

'Yes.'

McTavish remained silent for a long time. He moved away from Thomas and looked at him. 'Why?' he asked finally. 'Why did you do it?'

'There was something I had to do,' Thomas said, looking straight at him, 'or at least I thought I had to do it.'

McTavish ran his fingers down his big mustache. 'You didn't have to tell me this,' he said.

'There's more,' Thomas said, and he explained about the ten men who had escaped from the column and vowed they would kill him.

'How do you know about it?' McTavish asked.

Thomas told him about the man who died in his arms during the attack on Fort Stedman, and about how he had killed Mason in a gunfight aboard a river boat.

'Then there's eight more after your hide.'

'Yes.'

'And you think my hand might be one of them?'

'He could be, couldn't he?'

'Where did all that happen?' McTavish asked.

'West Virginia.'

'Bob said he was taken at Chickamauga,' McTavish told him. 'He was sent to Ohio.'

'Then I guess,' Thomas said, 'he's not going to be after my hide.'

Again there was a long silence between the two men, until McTavish asked, 'Would you do it again, Thomas?'

'I've thought a lot about it,' Thomas said, 'and under the same conditions I would do it again.'

'Even knowing what you know now?'

Thomas managed a smile. 'If that were so,' he answered, 'then things would not be the same as they were then…'

'You're a hard man, Thomas.'

'So I've been told.'

'But it takes a hard man,' McTavish told him, 'to drive north.'

Thomas nodded.

'I'll bring my herd up in the morning,' McTavish said.

McTavish, true to his word, came up with his herd just before Thomas decided to wait until it grew lighter before giving the order to throw the cows off their bedground. 'I got one thousand head,' the Scotsman bellowed as he rode into camp. 'My boys are holdin' them about a mile south of here.'

'Climb down and have some grub,' Thomas said, waving toward the cookfire.

'Don't mind if I do,' McTavish answered, swinging out of the saddle. 'This ain't no fit hour for a man to be runnin' around with a growling stomach.'

Thomas handed him a tin plate and cup and a fork and knife.

'Flapjacks and bacon and —' Victor started to tell him.

'Jest set the grub down on the plate,' McTavish laughed. 'I'll do my own pickin' and choosin'.'

Thomas and McTavish talked as they ate. McTavish said, 'My boys have their own remuda.'

'How many mounts?'

'Two dozen.'

'Could use more.'

'Can't spare them.'

Thomas nodded.

'Bob is one of the hands with the herd,' the Scotsman said.

'I'll take any man I can get,' Thomas answered, and then he told him that he was going to try to get to Kansas City or any other place where he could sell the herd.

'And what if you're forced back?' McTavish asked, biting into a hot biscuit.

'I'm sure as hell not planning on that,' Thomas said.

'Sometimes things happen that we don't exactly plan on happenin'.'

Thomas took a long swallow of hot coffee before he said, 'Those cattle will get to a market.'

'Suppose,' the Scotsman persisted, 'the way north is blocked—'

'I'm going to make it,' Thomas maintained stubbornly. He got to his feet and called out to Luke, 'Throw 'im off!'

McTavish took hold of Thomas' arm. 'Listen to me, will you? If you can't make it one way, you might be able to do it another. Say the way north is blocked. Okay, you swing the herd east, take them to the Mississippi, and load them on flatboats. The prices in New Orleans might be a shade less than up north, but whatever you get will be better than gettin' nothin'.'

'Flatboats?' Thomas questioned.

McTavish nodded.

Thomas rubbed his hand over the stubble on his chin.

'Jest think about it, Thomas,' McTavish told him. 'It might be a way to beat Wheeler and Johnson at their own game.'

Thomas' hand went to his gun. 'This is the only damn thing those bastards will ever understand.'

McTavish shrugged and commented, 'There's sometimes a way of beatin' a feller without havin' to kill him.'

'I haven't seen it yet,' Thomas said.

'The Good Book says, "Live by the sword, die by the sword".'

'It also says,' Thomas answered, "an eye for an eye, a tooth for a tooth".' Even to himself he sounded strangely like his father. He shook his head, as if to deny the similarity.

'I'll tell my boys to move the herd in close to yours. I suppose they'll be balky at first.'

'Aren't they all?' Thomas laughed. 'It's the nature of critters to be that way.'

The two men mounted up.

'I'll see you in a couple of months,' Thomas said, extending his hand across the space that separated their horses.

'Take care and good luck,' McTavish answered.

'Send my best to your wife. Next time I'll take dinner with you.'

'That's fine,' McTavish answered. 'That's really fine!'

Thomas swung his mount north, and without looking back he rode up to his segundo to give him word about McTavish's herd.

'My God,' Luke exclaimed, 'we're a real outfit now.'

Luke passed the order to the other drovers while Thomas rode lead. He looked back over his shoulder; the brown twist-horn was out in front. The rest of the cows were beginning to arrange themselves in a long column of twos and threes. The yellow flash of the sun flooded across the eastern sky, and the day began.

The morning passed to the slow steady movement of the herd. About noon Thomas told Luke to ride lead while he went back to see how McTavish's herd was doing.

'Give 'em a while longer on the trail,' he said, 'and then let 'em graze while we take time for grub.'

Luke nodded, and Thomas dropped back along the line of cows. About half a mile behind his drag rider, he met up with the two point men on McTavish's herd. They exchanged names and then he told them to let their cows graze with his. 'When we throw 'em on the trail again,' he said, 'they'll be mixed with mine and come along easily.'

The men nodded, and Thomas continued to drop back. One of the men riding swing was Bob. His full name was Bob Witter. He was a lean man of average height, with blond hair and cold blue eyes. He gestured with his hand when Thomas called out to him. If McTavish had said anything to him about the prison incident, he did not show it. Thomas repeated what he had told the point men, and rode on to give the word to the rest of the hands. By the time he returned to the chuck wagon, the herd was off the trail and grazing.

The riders came drifting in by twos, taking time to change horses, eat, and rest a bit before heading out to the herd again. Almost to a man they complained about the heat.

That afternoon, while the herd was still on the trail, huge clouds began to pile up to the north and west. But they were too far away to even promise rain for the parched range.

Because the two herds were mixed, the pace was slower. All of the drovers were busy keeping up the corners, and that meant a lot of riding, shouting, and back-beating to keep the cows in a column that was not strung out too long.

Hot and sweaty, the men made liberal use of their quirts, and more than once some steer started to run from the trail only to be chased and busted by a cursing rider. Toward evening Thomas found a good-sized stream, and that gave the men and the cows a chance to cool off.

McTavish's men were assigned to various positions along the column. Thomas, wherever possible, tried to pair one of his riders with one of McTavish's. And by the time the herd was bedded for the night, all the changes that had to be made were made.

The sunset flamed across the sky in a brilliant display of red, yellow, and orange, all of which deepened to a rich purple before the final cover of darkness set in. Those men who were not night herding talked for a while before stretching out to get a few hours' sleep.

Thomas rode around the herd, and for a few minutes he spoke with each of the men on the first watch of the night. Both told him that the herd was quiet. One said, 'It was plumb tuckered out.' And the other claimed, 'Those doggies are full up with grass and water.'

Probably each man was a little right. But Thomas nodded, accepting each statement as a verity, and, bidding each man good night, rode back to the chuck wagon.

'Any coffee left?' Thomas asked as he dismounted.

'I make a full pot,' Victor told him, 'so the riders comin' in an' goin' out can drink.'

Thomas chuckled. 'Victor, you'll turn out to be a first-rate trail cook yet,' he told the grinning man. 'Now why don't you turn in and get some sleep?'

'*Muchas gracias,*' Victor answered.

Thomas hunkered down close to the fire, smoked a cigarette, and slowly drank his coffee. Out from where the herd was bedded came the plaintive sound of one of the night herders singing to the cows. And from farther out on the range a chorus of howling coyotes started up. The clouds Thomas had seen at sunset were no longer in the northern sky. The night was very clear…

The sound of footsteps behind him made Thomas turn.

'Can't sleep none,' Bob said, coming up to the cook fire.

'There's a pot of coffee,' Thomas told him.

Bob helped himself to coffee and squatted down close to the fire. For a long while he looked into the flames without saying a word, though now and then he sipped at the coffee. Then, almost as if he were talking to himself, he said, 'I knowed a Carey once.'

Thomas' heart skipped a beat. He shifted the tin cup to his left hand and the right one eased toward his gun. But as soon as he realized the man was not armed, his right hand drifted to his lap.

'He wuz a lootenant. Got took by the Yankees at Chickamauga, like Mister McTavish's boy. The Yankees took a whole lot of us.' Bob nodded and tossed the remaining coffee grounds back of him. I disremember 'is first name, but some of those taken wid him called him Lootenant Carey. Hurt bad…' He looked across the low fire and asked, 'Any kin of you'n?'

'My brother Clem was reported missing there,' Thomas answered. That this drover might have run into Clem was possible, but —

'The McTavish boy is dead,' Bob told Thomas after another long silence, and then poured himself more coffee. When he had settled down near the fire again he said, 'Don't know if'n Lootenant Carey is alive. I busted out an' didn't meet up wid anyone who knowed 'im.'

'How bad was he hurt?'

'Took 'is left hand off.'

Thomas stared into the fire. His brother had always been something of a dandy, and for him to have lost an arm would have been a hard blow. It was hard for any man, but for someone like Clem, who put so much stock in the way he looked, well — Thomas shook his head.

'Tell ya,' Bob commented, ''e wuz a tough one, a real tough one. 'E hated Yankees more than any man I've come ag'inst.'

'Clem wasn't much of a hater,' Thomas said, 'and he wasn't tough.'

'Could be a different Carey,' Bob suggested as he got to his feet.

'Could be.'

'You in da war?' Bob asked.

'Yeah.'

'Thought so.'

'How come?'

'Puts a mark on a man, all that fightin' an' killin',' Bob said. 'Those dat has it can always see it on 'nother feller.' He put the cup down on the back counter of the chuck wagon. 'If'n he wuz your brother, ya can be right proud of 'im.'

Thomas nodded and asked, 'You sure about the McTavish boy?'

'I'm sure,' Bob answered flatly. 'I kilt 'im myself.'

'You what?' Thomas asked, scrambling to his feet.

'I come 'ere,' he said, ''cause Billy ast me to come 'fore 'e died … he wuz right fond of 'is folks an' didn't want 'em to grieve over 'im.'

'But why did you kill him?'

'Needed killin',' Bob answered.

He said it in such a way that Thomas found himself nodding. There was little doubt that Bob expected him to understand.

Though different from one another, they were similar enough to recognize that each lived by the same code.

'My turn at night herdin' soon,' Bob commented, and with that he slowly walked back to his sleeping roll.

Feeling suddenly chilled, Thomas hunkered close to the fire again and threw a few more pieces of cottonwood on it. Bob was sure a strange one, a very strange one. Though Thomas had some doubt as to whether the man had ever met a Lootenant Carey, he did not doubt for an instant that Bob had killed Billy McTavish.

TWELVE

Days passed, drifting into each other with the slow easy gait of the herd as it moved north. The heat was unrelenting. The faces of the men burned and blistered. Their lips dried, cracked, and bled. From sunrise to sundown the drovers ate dust and pressed the balky cows to keep moving. Red-eyed and with their strength sapped, the men did their work with a minimum of complaining.

Thomas soon got to know each man by name. McTavish's hands were younger by a good many years than those who were riding for him. But age did not matter on the trail. A man either did his job or drew his time and was sent packing.

Bob was the only man who caused Thomas some concern, though not because he failed to do his work. Bob was as good as, and sometimes better than, the other drovers. He was a skilled rider and an expert with rope. But after their talk, Thomas found himself watching the man.

He was a different breed all right, a loner, seldom speaking unless spoken to. There was something almost spooky about him, especially the way he prowled around the camp at night. He walked on the balls of his feet like a cat, sometimes coming around the side of the chuck wagon with such suddenness that Thomas, hearing his footsteps at the last moment, whirled around and almost threw down on him.

'Oughten to do that,' Thomas told him the third time it happened.

Bob nodded and his eyes went to slits, but he never said a word.

Thomas felt that the man was looking at the way he handled his gun. It almost seemed Bob was playing some sort of game, testing his quickness against Thomas' draw.

Even though Thomas recognized that Bob was not like the other men, he also found enough of himself in the man to be curious. On occasion, Thomas would signal Luke to come up and ride lead while he dropped back to talk to Bob, though he never did it without speaking to all of the other men. But the man never gave him too much leeway to get to know anything about him. Questions from Thomas seldom brought forth more than a 'yes' or a 'no.' And more often than not, the man would simply nod or shake his head.

Late one afternoon, after a hard day in a shimmering heat that played tricks on the eyes, putting clumps of trees where there were none and placid lakes where there was only sun-dried rangeland, Thomas reined in and signaled Luke to join him. In a matter of minutes his segundo came up.

'Think we'll be able to go till sundown?' Thomas asked.

Luke glanced back at the herd. 'Those are mighty hot cows,' he said.

'If we don't get some rain soon,' Thomas commented, 'they're goin' to be damn thirsty ones in a day or two.'

'Been noticin' the water is gettin' scarcer. Creek we stopped at this mornin' didn't have much life in it.'

'Those cows are going to get meaner than hell,' Thomas said, 'if they're going to have to go without water.'

'How far are we from the Brazos?'

'Two, three days.'

'Maybe we'll be lucky,' Luke suggested.

Thomas smiled. 'Maybe we will.'

Luke took another look at the herd. 'They seem to be goin' pretty good now. Seems a shame to stop them. Reckon we'll keep 'em movin' till then.'

Thomas nodded, and expected his segundo to swing around and ride back to the herd. But instead Luke remained where he was. 'Anything wrong?' he asked.

'I'm not sure, Mister Carey,' the man answered, looking off into the distance.

Thomas searched the horizon. There was nothing out there, not even any clouds. As far as to where the sky and the earth touched in any direction stretched the sun-baked rangeland.

'Did you ever hear anythin' about a whole wagon of gold, Confed'rate gold?' Luke asked.

'Some,' Thomas answered, looking at the man. 'But where'd *you* hear about it?'

'Hard to keep a story like that quiet,' Luke said.

Thomas agreed.

'One of the men thinks the gold is hereabouts, or is headin' here.'

'I heard that too,' Thomas said. 'But I sure as hell wouldn't put much stock in it.'

'I don't, but I think maybe some of the other boys are,' Luke told him. 'Especially since one of your kin —'

'My what?'

'You have a brother —'

'I had two,' Thomas said sharply.

'One named Clem?'

Thomas nodded.

'He's the one,' Luke said.

'He's the one what?' Thomas asked, anticipating what Luke was going to say and not knowing how to deny it.

'The one who's bringing the gold west.'

Thomas did not know whether to laugh or curse. Either reaction would have offended his segundo, and with a crazy rumor bothering the hands, that was the last thing he wanted to do. Drovers could get downright mean, and having his segundo all the way would be a hell of a lot better than not having him at all. 'Clem,' he started to explain, 'was taken at—'

'Chickamauga.'

'Yes.'

'I'm only tellin' you what was told to me.'

'If Clem is with the gold,' Thomas said, working to keep the edge out of his voice, 'I don't know anything about it. Clem was reported missing. I didn't even know he was taken prisoner till I was told, and I'm still not sure it was my brother who was in that Yankee prison.'

Luke rubbed his grizzled chin, and after a pause he asked, 'You don't put much stock in it, do you?'

'That's what I said,' Thomas responded. 'And mixing my brother in it doesn't make me change my mind.'

Luke nodded and said, 'Just thought you should know.'

'I'm beholden to you,' Thomas answered.

'Could be some truth to it?' his segundo ventured.

'Could be,' Thomas had to admit but then he quickly added, 'If there is, I don't know about it.'

'I'll pass the word to the men,' Luke said as he swung his mount around.

Thomas waited a few moments, and then he eased his own horse into a walk. Why Bob would want to bedevil the other men with such a wild story escaped him. But he was sure as hell going to get something of an answer from the man, or he would pay him his time and send him packing.

Thomas worked his mount into a trot and then spurred him into a gallop. He was angry that Clem had been used in the story, damn angry about it!

Thomas rode lead. His anger was as hot as the yellow burn of the late afternoon sun. Several times he considered riding back and settling matters with Bob then and there.

But the more Thomas thought about it, the more even-tempered he became, especially when he realized that finishing the drive was a great deal more important than his feelings about Bob. The man did his work, and that was all that mattered.

When Thomas recognized the change, he laughed out loud. There had been a time when he would have started a ruckus first and thought about things afterward. He wondered if he was going soft — or, perhaps even worse, afraid to have a showdown.

For a few moments he examined both possibilities, and with a shake of his head rejected them. Finishing the drive was more important than getting into a fight over foolish talk.

Though he was beginning to believe that somehow a band of men must have gotten a wagonload of gold out of Richmond before Grant's troops took the city, Thomas sure as hell was not ready to believe that Clem was involved in it. He did not even believe that Bob had met up with Clem in prison. After all, the man's word was less believable now that his story had Clem mixed up with the gold. But Thomas was still puzzled by the whole thing. It did not make sense why a man should spread a foolish story like that.

Thomas shrugged and rode on.

Twilight came on, sheeting the western sky with curtains of flaming clouds, and there were dark ones building up tall as mountains to the north. The herd was bedded down, but jittery enough to keep the men fathering it busy. There was a peculiar stillness on the range. The air was heavy and smelled of burning sulfur. Even the remuda was restless.

Thomas rode up to the chuck wagon, swung off his mount, and, turning it over to the wrangler, said, 'Better keep a couple of changes for the men handy. The critters are skittish as hell.'

The man nodded but did not answer.

Thomas hunkered down to the fire. Suddenly he sensed something was wrong. Prickles raced down his back, the way they did whenever he was close to some danger. His first impulse was to stand and, if not draw his gun, at least be ready to. But he remained where he was, poured a cup of coffee, and then stood up.

The drovers were ranged in a small semicircle on the other side of the cook fire. Luke was on the right, a man named Cole was on the left, and Bob was almost in the center. Bob was armed. His six-gun was low on his right hip with the holster tied.

Thomas sipped his coffee and said, 'We should make the Brazos in two, maybe three, days.'

None of the men moved, and then Bob stepped out in front of them and said, 'We ain't a-goin' to th' Brazos.'

'That's the way the trail goes,' Thomas answered, keeping calm.

Some of the drovers snickered.

Bob gestured to the men and said, 'They're not interested in herdin' cows when they can live nice an' easy on gold. I done tol' 'em about your brother Clem.'

Thomas started to shift his cup from the right to the left hand.

'Better not try, Mister Carey,' Bob said, his gun leaping free of the holster. 'I done learned your ways.'

'So you have,' Thomas answered. 'But you and the others here signed on to drive the herd.'

'That's a-fore they knowed about the gold,' Bob responded.

'If there is gold —'

'There's gold, all right!' Bob exclaimed.

'An' your brother is bringin' it out here for you an' him to split up,' one of the other men said.

'Better drop your gun belt,' Bob said.

Thomas unbuckled the belt and let it fall to the ground.

'Now we can talk,' Bob told him.

'There's nothing to talk about,' Thomas said, dropping his coffee cup. 'I haven't seen my brother since the war began. Last I heard, he was missing.'

'Shit, man,' one of the riders exploded. 'Bob 'ere met up with 'im in prison.'

'Maybe,' Thomas said, 'but if he was in prison, then how the hell did he get the gold?'

'He busted out,' Bob said.

Thomas looked at him questioningly. 'You didn't tell me that.'

'He busted out with me —'

'You said you didn't see him or even hear about him after you got out.'

'He busted out with me. We went back ta Virginia. Or Clem bein' an officer got himself a mighty sweet an' soft job. Officer in charge of I forgets what it's callt, but it's the place wherein the gold is kept. I was sent back to do some more fightin'. But 'fore I leave I meets of Clem again an' he says ta me, he does, "If'n you make it through this shindig, come out to Texas. I owe you an' I mean to pay." Next thin' the fightin's done, an' I heard about the gold. I damn well know Clem has his hand in it somehow. And that's the gospel truth. I figure ta get what 'e owes me fer savin' 'is life when I took him with me when I busted out...'

Thomas nodded. This time he knew the story was true, because it was too involved for Bob to have made up. 'What about McTavish's boy?' he asked.

'He went wid us,' Bob answered. 'But like I already tol' ya, he needed killin', an' like I tol' you, I come to his folks 'cause that was his dyin' wish. I expected to 'ead down your way in a little while, but you saved me the trouble by comin' to me.'

Thomas nodded. 'I guess we'd have met sooner or later.'

'Likely,' Bob agreed.

'Tell 'im what's on yer mind,' one of the men said. A few agreed.

To Thomas the men did not look any different from any other drovers. They were streaked with grime and wet with sweat. Their duds needed a good washing and they smelled sour. They were hard men, and like the rest of their kind they were strong, pitting their strength and skill against a longhorn. But for all their look-alike, these were different. They were no longer interested in making it to Dodge with the herd. They wanted the easy life, and the gold to buy it...

'The way I sees it,' Bob said, 'you ain't just trailin' a herd, your fixin' ta meet up wid Clem —'

'You're wrong!'

'Don't figger I am. Takin' a herd north this time of the year is plumb wrong; ever'body knows that. Sure, you gotta sell off some cows. Take 'em to New Orleans or down to Gulf Port. But not north with injuns runnin' all over and rus'lers a-waitin' for your...' Bob shook his head. 'Like I says, you is fixin' ta meet up with ol' Clem. And we'll be with you when you meet 'im.'

The men in the semicircle quickly voiced their agreement.

'Then you're going to be with me until hell freezes over,' Thomas answered.

'Nary as long as that,' Bob said.

'What about the herd?' Thomas questioned.

'Up on that Brazos there be them that'll take it,' Bob said. 'A feller callt Johnson is up there. What he can't buy his men'll take. He'll pay ten dollars a 'ead —'

'And get four, five times that,' Thomas said angrily.

Bob shrugged.

'It's not cows we're interested in,' one of the other drovers called out. 'It's gold.'

'I'll do the talkin',' Bob told the man, turning to look at him.

'The whole lot of you,' Thomas said, 'are damn fools. You're listening to one man's story. Now listen to this. My brother was reported missing and I never received word that he was found or taken prisoner or anything else. And I sure as hell wouldn't know if he was coming this way with ten wagonloads of gold...'

'He a-lyin' to you,' Bob shouted. 'He's a-lyin' —'

'Thomas!' Luke shouted, tossing him a gun.

Bob turned toward the segundo, but the gun had already left the man's hand. Two shots exploded in the deep twilight stillness. Luke was dead before he hit the ground.

Bob whirled around with his gun blazing.

Thomas leaped off to the side, out of Bob's line of fire, and from a crouch he squeezed the trigger.

Bob screamed as the slug tore off his right arm just below the elbow. His hand, still holding the gun, lay on the dusty range, while blood poured out of the bloody stump. He dropped to his knees.

'For God sakes,' he wailed, 'I tol' you the truth!'

Thomas squeezed the trigger. The slug tore into Bob's chest, and as he sprawled sideways the earth began to tremble.

Everything was suspended, and then one of the men shouted, 'Boys, the cattle's runnin'!'

In an instant all hands were running for their horses. Thomas was mounted and racing toward the herd. The cows must have heard the shooting and took off. There were riders following close behind…

Thomas glanced up. Darkness had come sometime back. The sky was covered with heavy clouds. Even as Thomas lowered his gaze, a bolt of lightning shot across the sky. The thunder followed, making it feel as if the earth were shaking itself to pieces.

A large part of the herd wheeled away from the lightning, while the other part kept on running toward it.

Lightning was suddenly streaking all over the sky, and the claps of the thunder that followed close behind each other merged into a hellish drum roll. The wind suddenly sprang up, blowing the dust off the range, forcing the men to protect their faces from its sharp sting.

Thomas and some of the drovers followed the part of the herd that veered away from the lightning. They gained on them. There was fox fire playing on the longhorns, and someone yelled that it was running around the rim of Thomas' hat…

Ropes of lightning twisted through the sky while salvo after salvo of thunder broke over the running herd.

The wind turned cold, and just as Thomas raced out in front of the lead cows the rain hit them. It gushed as though a wall of water had been cracked apart by the sharp blows of thunder. It struck the men with a savage force, bending them low over their horses.

The cows were still pounding forward, their hooves making a sound like thunder that came from deep within the earth, and their frightened bellowing mixed with the wild sounds of the storm. They ran with their horns cracking together and the dull thud of their bodies smashing into each other.

Thomas was yelling at the top of his lungs, trying to bring the lead cow around and get the rest to follow into some sort of a mill. But each time he came in close to the charging animal, the critter dodged off to one side and then plunged wildly ahead.

'Hey, cow!' he shouted into the teeth of the wind and rain. 'Ho, cow!' But the fury of the storm crushed his words the instant they were out of his mouth.

The streaks of lightning lessened, and soon became no more than flickers to the east and south. The thunder diminished to an angry roll. But the cold rain, still driven by the wind, slashed at the running herd and the men who were desperately trying to bring the herd under their control.

'Try turning them with the slicker,' Thomas yelled to the rider behind him as he worked himself free from the saddle. Moments later he whipped the yellow coat out to the side of him and ran his mount close to the lead cow.

Flailing the slicker in front of the running steer's face and yelling 'Turn, you fucker, turn! Turn, you fucker, turn!' Thomas took the desperate chance of cutting his horse across the wild cow's path.

The cow bobbed his head to avoid the brush of the slicker. One of his horns caught Thomas in the thigh and dug a furrow into it.

'Turn, you bastard!' Thomas shouted, feeling the searing pain of the gouge. 'Turn!'

The cow suddenly faltered and swung away to his left.

Thomas went after him, and before the critter had a chance to get set for another run, he whipped the cow with his slicker.

The critter turned again. He was running back toward the herd, and the cows behind him were following.

'Keep 'em coming,' Thomas shouted at the other riders. 'Keep working them tighter and tighter. I'm going over to see how the rest of the bunch is doing.'

He swung away from the mill and galloped back to find the other part of the herd. He found it some miles to the south. The cows were milling but under control.

'We'll hold 'em to daybreak,' Thomas told the wet drovers, 'then we'll bring the two parts together.'

None of the men answered, and Thomas knew there was nothing they could say. He rode back to camp and hoped that Victor had started to dig the graves for the two dead men.

THIRTEEN

The morning rose gray and wet. The men stayed with the herd while Victor tended to burying Luke and Bob. Thomas stood by and watched as each man was lowered into a shallow muddy grave.

'You goin' to say words over them?' Victor asked when he had finished filling Luke's grave.

'None to say,' Thomas answered, and he limped back to the chuck wagon. He had liked and respected Luke, but nothing he could say over the man's grave would make him rise up like a second Lazarus. As for Bob, the man was a damn fool to think that he could —

Thomas shook his head. It made little sense to waste time thinking about Bob. Sooner or later he would have gotten himself killed. His kind always did!

But Thomas did think about Clem. He no longer doubted there was a wagonload of gold, and from the details Bob had given him that his brother was involved in its removal from Richmond. Yet in some ways he still found it hard to believe. Clem was the real gentleman in the family. He had no use for the ranch, and William had sent him north to study law at Yale University. Clem was also the only one who had believed in the Confederacy and what it stood for, even to buying black women for his pleasure and then selling them when he no longer wanted them.

But whatever Clem was, he was not tough, at least not in the sense that hard work gave a man physical strength; and he was not a fighter, either with his hands or with a gun. And yet, if any man could take gold out of Richmond and head it west, Thomas had absolutely no doubt that his brother could. Clem was smart — not book smart the way John was, but smart like William.

Father and son had had a lot in common. William had driven a hard bargain; he had been bound to come out better than the other fellow in any business dealings. Clem was much the same way. He was always scheming, pitting his wits against another man. He had a good head on his shoulders, and more than likely the war had toughened him. It did that to most men. They either hardened or they died. Those were the only two choices.

Thomas hoisted himself up on to the driver's seat and scrambled under the protection of the canvas covering. For a few minutes he tended the gash in his thigh. It was a good-sized furrow, and even with the Indian-type dressing on it, healing would be slow. Luckily, none of the muscle had been cut, but it throbbed like hell and was God-awful stiff.

Victor clambered on to the driver's seat and, poking his head into the gloomy shell of the wagon, he said, 'I'm ready to move out. I got your mount saddled and hitched up to the side.'

'Go ahead,' Thomas answered. 'Move!'

Victor yelled at the mules and snapped the bullwhip over their backs. The animals strained at the traces and slowly, with a great deal of creaking and more shouting from Victor, the chuck wagon broke free from the suck of mud and began its jouncing movement.

'Better have the cows go over the graves or them *duo hombres* are goin' to be food for wolves,' Victor said, looking into the wagon again.

'I intend to,' Thomas answered.

'What you do for a segundo?'

'Pick one soon enough.'

Victor nodded.

'Don't plan to go much today,' Thomas told him. 'Just head up a ways. Maybe three, four miles. Then make some grub. I'll send the hands back in pairs.'

'Think there'll be more trouble?'

'Not from the men,' Thomas answered. 'They've had just about all the trouble they want.'

'Seein' a killin' or two always makes a man stop and think.'

'Sure as hell does,' Thomas agreed, climbing out of the wagon and sitting down next to Victor.

'How's your thigh?'

'Could be a lot worse,' Thomas told him, scanning the leaden skies. 'Looks like we're going to have rain for a while.'

'If it rains much more,' Victor commented, 'the Brazos will come to us. We won't have to drive them cows to it.'

Thomas did not answer. Either there was not enough rain and a man burned in the sun and ate dust, or the rain came with bone-chilling swiftness and continued to fall until the range was nothing but mud, and the men too wet and cold to be anything but hair-trigger touchy.

'What you goin' to do about that Johnson *hombre*?' Victor asked.

'I've been thinking on it,' Thomas said.

Victor glanced at him.

'He has *mucho pistoleros*.'

'I don't want a fight,' Thomas said. 'But that son-of-a-bitch has been sticking in my craw for a long time now. I guess it's about time to pull him out.'

'You goin' to gun for him?'

Thomas shrugged, and in a low voice he said, 'I have a score to settle with him.' He looked at Victor. 'I'm sure as hell not going to sell one cow of this herd to him, not at the price he was offering.'

'No, by God,' Victor exclaimed, 'this herd goes to KC!'

Thomas reached back to where his mount was tethered, freed it, and eased alongside of the driver's seat. When he was in the saddle, he asked, 'Think you can get some hot grub going?'

'I'll do what I can,' Victor assured him.

Thomas eased his mount away from the wagon and then, swinging around, rode south through the rain to the nearest bunch of cows. It was just becoming light enough for him to see where the lead of the sky fit close against the brown of the earth.

Thomas rode up to the first bunch of cows. The men had held them in a tight mill throughout the night. The critters looked as if they did not have any more run in them, but he knew all too well that cows could be deceiving that way.

He circled the bunch until he saw Dodd, a compact man who had an easy way with the cows. Dodd was one of McTavish's hands and, with the exception of Bob, probably the best roper among them.

Thomas waved for the man to join him.

'They look quiet enough,' Thomas said, bringing his horse to a halt in front of Dodd.

'Wouldn't trust 'em none,' the man commented.

'From now on,' Thomas told him, 'you're segundo.'

The role of straw boss did not sit well with him, and he said so.

'There's no one else,' Thomas said.

Dodd named some of the other men. 'They're a damn sight more experienced than me.'

'Might be,' Thomas said, shifting in his saddle to look over the cows, 'but I want you to be my segundo.'

'Don't see why —'

'You're it,' Thomas told him. 'I'll pass the word to the other men. Now I want a trail count made.'

'Yes, Mister Carey,' Dodd answered.

Thomas was about to turn and ride away but the man said, 'I'm right sorry about what happened last night. Luke was a good man, and if I'd-a knowed Bob meant to turn it into a killing business, then I'd have never stood with him.'

Thomas' eyes went to slits. 'No one ever thinks that something is going to turn into a killing business,' he said, 'but they sure as hell should, especially if they're holding a gun.'

The new segundo nodded.

'Once the herd is formed up, take 'em over the graves,' Thomas said. 'Might be the best place to count 'em.

'I'll start throwing these critters on the trail,' Dodd told him.

'See you in a while,' Thomas said, and rode farther south, to the second bunch of cows. He told each man that Dodd was his segundo, and the men either nodded or mumbled, 'He's a good one for the job.'

By noon the men had been fed some hot grub, or at least lukewarm grub, and a trail count had been made.

'Seems like we got a hundred fifty more head than when we started,' Dodd told Thomas as the two of them circled the herd, which had been moved near the chuck wagon but no farther.

'Any brands on 'em?'

'Not so as a man could see right quick,' the segundo answered.

'We'll take them along,' Thomas said, 'and when I sell 'em off I'll divvy up with the boys what those hundred and fifty head'll bring.'

'That's a lot of money, Mister Carey.'

'Six thousand dollars.'

'Are you thinkin' we're goin' to have trouble at the Brazos?' Dodd asked after a long pause.

'I'm hoping we're not,' Thomas replied.

The other man nodded.

It rained for the rest of the day and all that night. But by first light the sky was clear, and when the sun had swung over the eastern rim of the range it was hot and yellow.

Thomas let the herd graze for a few days, giving the men a chance to rest up and dry out. When they were on the trail again they covered ten miles before the herd was bedded for the night. On the second and third days they moved as well.

Toward noon on the fourth day Thomas caught sight of two riders off in the southwest. They were too far away to tell whether they were Indians or not. But when the men came in for grub, he warned them to be on the lookout. And before Thomas rode out to take up the lead for the afternoon's drive, he told Dodd, 'Ride up and down the length of the herd for the rest of the day. I don't want any surprises.'

'How long do you think they've been trailin' us?' Dodd asked.

'Most of the morning,' Thomas answered. 'They probably started on the east side of us and swung around with the sun.'

'Be hard as hell to see them come late afternoon,' the segundo commented.

Thomas nodded, lifted up his saddle, and walked over to the remuda for a fresh mount. Later, when he was out in front of the herd, he rode up to the top of a small knoll and searched for the riders. But there was no sign of them.

By the time most of the afternoon had passed, Thomas was fairly certain that the riders either had broken off trailing the herd or had swung around to the front. And though he fretted about the second possibility, there was not a damn thing he could do about it without changing the direction in which the herd was moving.

The sun was well to Thomas' left, and was just beginning to drift below the horizon. In another hour or so the sky would flame into a blaze of color. It was time to look for a good bed ground. He saw a fine level stretch about a half mile ahead.

Thomas trotted up to it and waited. When he saw the point riders he would signal Dodd to throw the herd off the trail. But in the meantime he fixed a cigarette and slouched easy in the saddle as he smoked. Before he realized it, two riders were coming toward him. They were Indians.

Thomas eased himself up, ready to go for his gun. But as the Indians came closer, he saw that one of them took the lead and that his hand was raised in a gesture of peace. These Indians were not his enemy.

Thomas made the same gesture.

The Indians brought their ponies to a halt some ten paces in front of Thomas. One was no more than a boy. The other was an older man, at least fifty years old. He was lean and muscular. The reddish glow of a dying sun played over his bare chest. He was as tall as Thomas, and his face looked as though it had been chiseled out of dark rock, the kind found on the banks of the Colorado.

The elder of the two said something in their native tongue.

'My father, Red Tail,' the boy haltingly translated into English, 'asks if you have white man's medicine?'

Thinking the Indian wanted whiskey, Thomas shook his head and answered, 'Tell your father Red Tail that I come with the herd —'

Red Tail spoke again.

'He says white man's medicine is very strong. He says his daughter needs very strong medicine to overcome the evil spirit. He says daughter will go soon to the spirit land.'

'What's wrong with the young squaw?'

The boy spoke to his father and Red Tail answered, gesturing off to the southwest.

Thomas understood, and without waiting for the boy to translate, he said, 'I will look at the squaw and see if white man's medicine will help her. But first I must take care of the herd.'

The young Indian quickly told his father what was said, and when he was finished the man spoke to Thomas in sign language, telling him that he would wait for him.

Thomas nodded and tossed his small bag of tobacco to the boy and, wheeling around, rode back to the herd, which was less than half a mile away. He came up to his segundo and, doubling back, came alongside of him.

'There's bed ground,' he said, 'not too far ahead. Get the herd set for the night. There're two Indians up a ways. Seems like there's a sick squaw not far from here. I'll go over and take a look.'

'Alone?' Dodd asked.

Thomas considered the question.

'There might not be a sick squaw there,' Dodd said.

'Might not,' Thomas agreed with a nod and asked, 'Who's handy with a gun?'

'Flood,' the segundo answered. 'He's flank man.'

'Send him up,' Thomas said, and he trotted ahead before spurring his mount into a gallop. By the time he reached the Indians, Flood was coming up fast. 'Tell your father,' Thomas explained to the boy, 'that one of my men is coming with me.'

Red Tail was glowering by the time his son finished translating.

'Tell him,' Thomas said, 'I will help the young squaw if I can.'

The elder man spoke.

'He says —' the boy started, and, breaking off, he spoke to his father.

Flood came up and reined in. He was a rangy man with sharp brown eyes that looked questioningly at Thomas.

'The old man doesn't like the idea of your coming with me,' Thomas explained.

The elder man spoke again.

'He says,' the boy told them, 'that he comes for white medicine because Indian medicine has no power against the bullet that came from a white gun.'

'What's he talkin' about?' Flood asked, leaning close to Thomas.

'I think the squaw was shot.'

'You sure you know what you're doin', Mister Carey?'

'I won't know,' Thomas answered, 'until I do it.'

The older man motioned to them and then trotted off to the southwest.

'I guess we follow,' Thomas said.

'Come!' called the boy as he rode after his father.

'Sure changed his mind fast enough,' Flood commented as he and Thomas trailed behind the Indians.

'He said his piece and that was the end of it.'

'Might be the end of us too,' Flood commented.

There was more truth to what Flood said than Thomas wanted to admit. Going off after some Cheyennes was a foolish thing to do, and yet, if he had not agreed to go, the consequences might have been bad enough to make him wish he had. The herd could be stampeded. They could pick off men, and if there were any more braves in Red Tail's camp they could —

'Sun's almost down,' Flood said.

'It'll be a good clear night again,' Thomas answered. 'We should make the river by week's end.'

Flood took a bite out of a plug of tobacco, pushing the wad in the pouch of his cheek before he said, 'We've made good time. I'm thinkin' we'll get to KC 'fore the snow comes.'

'I sure as hell hope so!'

'If we don't, it's not for want of tryin'.'

The sun was gone, and all that remained of it was a strip of blood-red cloud. When that, too, faded, the black sky filled with stars.

Thomas noticed that there was a slope to the land, and mentioned it to Flood.

'We've come aways from the herd,' the man answered.

They continued without speaking for a while longer, and then the young boy looked back at them and said, 'Wickiup there on the rise.' He pointed slightly off to the left. The Indians broke into a gallop. Thomas and Flood raced right behind them.

Thomas entered the wickiup and motioned Flood to wait outside. Inside the shelter the yellowish-red light from a small fire flickered over the face of the young squaw. Her face was beaded with sweat, and her rapid breathing thrust her young full breasts against her skin dress.

Red Tail spoke and the boy said, 'Bullet inside.' And he placed his hand just beneath his right breast.

Thomas put his hand on the squaw's forehead. It was hot with fever.

Her eyelids fluttered and opened. Fear rushed into her black eyes, and she uttered a small cry.

Red Tail spoke. The squaw shook her head. Red Tail spoke again, repeating what he had said.

'Don't know,' Thomas told the boy. 'How long has she been sick?'

The boy counted off five on his fingers and said, 'As many suns.'

'The slug has to come out.'

The boy quickly told his father what Thomas had said.

'And then there's no way of knowing whether she'll live or die.'

Red Tail listened to what his son had to say; then he spoke and the boy said, 'Take the slug out.'

Thomas explained that the squaw would be in pain when he cut the skin and drew blood. He also told them he must have a better fire and hot water. Then he said, 'The squaw must be tied so she can't move when I take the bullet from her.'

Red Tail spoke to the girl, and she started to whimper.

'How'd it happen?' Thomas asked, looking at the boy.

'White man —'

Red Tail said something, and from the tone of it Thomas knew he would get no more information from the boy.

'No hurt,' the squaw whispered.

Surprised that the girl spoke English, Thomas shook his head and answered, 'I'll do the best I can…'

Red Tail spoke again, and the young boy bound his sister Comanche-style, spread-eagled, as though she were a captive whom they were about to torture.

Thomas stepped outside of the wickiup and told Flood what was happening. 'I've taken slugs out of the shoulders or legs of men, but never out of a woman.'

'Where is it?'

'Below the right tit.'

Flood snorted and with a grin he said, 'Be mighty careful you don't slice none of her titty off, or she'll be kind of a lopsided squaw.'

'When those two bucks come out,' Thomas told his hand, 'I want you to keep them from coming back in. She's going to do a lot of yelling, and they just might get nervous.'

'They'll stay out,' Flood assured him.

'Don't shoot,' Thomas said, 'unless they rush you. Understand?'

The man nodded.

Thomas glanced at the sky. The moon had come up and dimmed most of the stars. 'It's going to be a long night,' he said.

The fire in the wickiup was brighter, and there was a pot of hot water within easy reach. Red Tail was softly singing to himself.

'Outside,' Thomas said, gesturing to the opening in the side of the shelter. 'Outside.'

Red Tail did not want to go.

'Tell him,' Thomas said, 'I will not work with him here.'

The boy translated.

Red Tail grumbled as he shuffled out.

'He says,' the boy told him, 'if squaw dies, you die.'

'Tell him,' Thomas answered hotly, 'to stop blowing wind from his mouth.'

The boy laughed and stepped after his father.

Thomas gave his attention to the girl. 'My name is Thomas,' he said, slipping his Bowie knife from its sheath. 'Thomas,' he repeated.

The girl nodded.

'You?'

'Small Flower,' she said.

He removed his wipe, and before Small Flower could scream, he gagged her.

She began to thrash.

Thomas tightened her bonds. Then, bending over her, he cut away her dress, exposing her body. He sucked in his breath. Her breasts were not much bigger than the span of his hand, her stomach was flat, and the dark hair of her womanhood was soft and silky-looking.

His eyes fastened on the wound. It was red and already festered. Quickly he removed his jacket, took off his shirt, and cut the back of it into strips. He put the pieces of cloth into the boiling water, took one out, and laid it against the wound.

The girl winced.

Thomas cleaned the hole as well as he could, and then he heated the point of his Bowie knife. When it was cherry red, he plunged it into the hot water, sending a small cloud of steam into the air.

'Okay,' he said in a low voice, 'I'm going to try to take the bullet out.'

He made a quick cut just below her breast. The girl strained against her rawhide bonds. She groaned, and the high-pitched scream in her throat was muffled by the gag.

Thomas widened the cut he had made. Putting his hands on the squaw's trembling body, he worked the lips of the incision even farther apart.

He wiped the sweat from his forehead with the back of his hand. The light from the fire was dying again, and he threw two more pieces of wood on it.

'The slug is not deep,' he told the girl. 'I'll be able to dig it out, but it's going to hurt.'

A wild look came back into her bright black eyes.

He reached up and touched her face. 'Don't blame you a bit for being scared, I'll try to make it as quick as possible.'

The wildness went out of the girl's eyes.

Picking up his Bowie knife, he set about digging the slug out. 'It's against one of your ribs. Lucky it was about spent before you got hit.'

The girl sucked in her breath and clenched her teeth.

Thomas suddenly realized she was trying hard not to move, not to make a sound. 'You're gutsy,' he said, working the sharp point around the slug, 'gutsy as hell.'

He stopped to let his own breathing come back to normal and wipe the sweat from his forehead again.

From outside the wickiup he could hear Red Tail getting louder and louder, and each time the Indian said something Flood answered with, 'Now you jest rest easy like, Red Tail, or I'll have to blow your fuckin' head off. Now you tell me what the hell kind of a Comanche are you goin' to be without your fuckin' head? No kind, I'm a-thinkin', no kind a-tall.'

Thomas smiled. Flood sure had a funny way of using words. 'Well,' Thomas said, 'just a bit more poking around and I should have it.' He touched the top of her head and ran his hand down her cheek. Even as he spoke he took the knife and pushed its point under the slug.

He glanced at her. Tears were skidding down her high dark cheekbones.

'No need to do that,' Thomas said quietly, realizing it was shame that brought the tears to the girl's eyes. 'I got to go a bit deeper,' he told her. The next instant he slipped the knife under the slug, and with his fingers he grabbed hold of it. 'Got it!' he shouted. 'I got the bastard!'

He held the stubby piece of metal up for the squaw to see, but she had already passed out. Thomas removed his wipe from her mouth and splashed water in her face.

She opened her eyes.

'All done,' he told her, and began tending the wound.

'No die?' Small Flower asked, weaker.

'Maybe not,' he answered. 'But you're still one sick squaw.' Thomas washed the wound, pinched it together, and said, 'When it's all better it'll leave a mark.'

The squaw nodded.

With the rest of his shirt he made a bandage. 'Change the bandage and wash the hole with hot water every day,' he told her. 'I'll get Red Tail —'

'You good man, Thomas,' she said, taking hold of his hand. She put his hand on her naked breast.

Thomas pulled it away.

She took hold of it again and said, 'You Thomas. Small Flower owe life. Small Flower belong to Thomas.'

With his free hand he touched her cheek and, bending over her, he kissed her forehead. 'I'll get your daddy now,' he said. A moment later he called out, 'Okay, Flood, let them pass.'

'Sure enough, Mister Carey.'

Red Tail and his son entered the wickiup. He looked at Little Flower and at Thomas.

'The slug is out,' Thomas said, and handed it to him.

Red Tail looked at his daughter again, and in a low voice he said, 'She live.'

'Well, I'll be a son-of-a-bitch,' Flood exclaimed. 'He talks!'

Red Tail nodded and said, 'Sometimes.'

'I swear,' Flood commented, 'there's no figurin' what an injun will do.'

'No figurin',' Red Tail said, 'what a white-eyes will do.' And he placed his hand on Thomas' bare shoulder. 'We smoke now…'

Sometime later Thomas rode back to the herd. But before he left the wickiup, he told Red Tail to come the next day and he would give him two beeves for Small Flower.

'Think the squaw'll live?' Flood asked when they were near the herd.

'I'm hoping she will,' Thomas answered wistfully. 'She's as gutsy as they come.'

FOURTEEN

Thomas and his drovers moved the herd north toward the Brazos. The cows were trail-broken, and at night bedded down without giving the hands too much trouble.

Each new day was not much different from the one that had passed. The sun was hot and the work hard. The dust and the sound of the cows was always in the air. The men, however different from one another, became knitted together into one of the best groups of drovers Thomas had ever seen. Much of the credit for this belonged to Dodd, his new segundo. The man had a real talent for handling cows, and the other hands were quick to realize it.

From time to time Indians were spotted on the flanks of the herd. But they kept close to the horizon. Thomas was sure they were Comanche, and though some of the men were jittery because of their presence, Thomas told them they might have more to worry about from Johnson than they did from the Indians.

The men spoke a lot about Thomas' experience with Red Tail, and Flood retold the story of how 'the boss saved that young squaw's life.' Each time he recited the story Flood added a bit more. 'Kinda juices it up,' he explained when Thomas questioned him about it.

If the hands were not listening to Flood, they were more than likely talking about the women they had loved. From reminiscing the men always went to describing the women they would have when they reached Kansas City. True to their kind, they spoke broadly about whoring and drinking. But they were boasting, and several of them were honest enough to admit it.

Thomas seldom listened to the conversation that took place around the cookfire at night. But now and then he would remember the times he had spent with Lisa, and the heat would begin to stir in his groin.

That love was gone now. It was gone when Lisa had married, and now that she held him responsible for her brother's death there was no way to bring it back. Yet Thomas had to admit he probably still loved her, at least in the way a man loved a woman when it came to wanting her in bed.

Sometimes Thomas' thoughts moved from Lisa to Helen. His relationship with her had become much more physical than it had ever been before he had left on the drive. And though he had become immensely fond of her, there was still something lacking. He was most keenly aware of the lack when his sex was sheathed in hers. The lack, though, he admitted, was in himself and not in her.

That realization never made Thomas feel any better. If it did anything, it made him realize how much he had made Helen suffer. And then, like the sudden onset of a summer storm, the black anger would come, making Thomas rage against himself, against her, and against William, who had brought it all to pass so many years before. At such times, he would gallop out to the herd, knowing that he was working out of his dark mood.

Thomas was at the Brazos about an hour before the herd came up. The river was brown with mud, and swift, but it was not nearly as swollen as he had feared it might be. He found a good crossing a half-mile downstream, where the river was no more than fifty yards across.

The south bank had a gentle slope to the water's edge, but the opposite side was much steeper. The men would have to keep the cows moving once they reached the other bank, or they would start climbing over each other. Fording the river would not be difficult, and there was probably ten yards or so that the cows would have to swim. Satisfied that the crossing could be made with a minimum of trouble, Thomas decided to throw the herd off the trail and make the crossing after the men had had a chance to eat and rest. That would also give him time to look around. So far he had not seen anything of Johnson's men. The only strangers were the Indians on the flanks of the herd. And by now they were no longer strangers. The men had begun to nickname the ones they saw.

Thomas rode back to the trail and waited for the herd. When Dodd came into view, he signaled him to throw the cows off the trail while he crossed the river and went up the opposite side. For the better part of an hour Thomas scouted in both directions along the bank. He saw nothing to indicate that a large group of men was in the immediate vicinity. Thomas recrossed the river, and when he came up to the chuck wagon he saw that some dozen riders had come galloping out of the south.

'Trouble!' he exclaimed, leaping from his horse.

'Sure looks like it,' Dodd answered.

The men were already racing for their carbines.

'We could make a fight of it,' Flood called out.

Before Thomas could answer, four of the oncoming riders swung away from the main body and went toward the herd.

One of the drovers leaped on his horse, and as he spurred the animal into a gallop, he shouted, 'I'm goin' to warn the others.'

'Gives us one less gun here,' Thomas said.

Dodd nodded.

'Put two men behind the chuck wagon,' Thomas told his segundo. 'Spread out the rest of them and don't fire unless I do.'

The riders were coming up fast and the dust rose like a pale-yellow flower over them. When they were close enough to see that the drovers were holding carbines, the front rider signaled the rest of them to slow down.

Thomas recognized him and shouted, 'That's close enough, Wheeler!'

Wheeler brought his mount to a trembling halt.

'You don't stand a chance!' Wheeler yelled.

Several shots came from the direction of the herd.

The earth began to tremble.

'Cattle's runnin'!' a drover shouted, and started for his horse.

'Stay put,' Thomas ordered. 'Stay put!'

'I warned you,' Wheeler said, 'not to start this damn drive.'

Thomas saw the sudden bloom of yellow dust against the blue sky. Too much had gone into bringing the herd into the Brazos to let anyone stop him from finishing the drive.

'Listen, Carey,' the man behind Wheeler called out, 'I'll give you five dollars a head right here and now.'

'Who are you?' Thomas answered, looking hard at the man, whose face was hidden by the shadow of his hat's wide brim.

'Name is Johnson, Bob Johnson,' the man answered. He rode past Wheeler and reined in when he was much closer to Thomas. 'Haven't I seen you before?' he asked, pushing back his hat.

'On a river boat,' Thomas answered with a nod, recognizing the heavy-set, bull-necked man.

'Why, sure!' Johnson exclaimed. 'I was standing at the bar. But weren't you traveling with an old guy and a baby —'

'My grandfather and my son,' Thomas said flatly.

Johnson's big face splintered into a grin. 'Carey, you're funnin' me. I knew your pa.'

'I know you did.'

The man's big face became serious and he asked, 'How?'

'I killed Zeb,' Thomas said. 'He told me you were the middleman between my father and Zeb.'

Johnson nodded. 'I figured something like that must have happened to Zeb,' he said, 'when I heard you were back.'

'Did you figure that when I met up with you I'd kill you?' Thomas asked, his voice casually pleasant. But even as he spoke, his right hand moved as his gun leaped from its holster. 'Now easy, Johnson, real easy, or I'll blow you apart. Climb down.'

'Carey,' Wheeler yelled, 'you don't have enough guns to back you.'

'I got the one that counts,' Thomas answered. 'Just stay where you are, Wheeler. Flood, take another man and get their guns. First man who tries to stop you, kill him!'

'There's more of us not far from here,' Wheeler told him.

'Tie them,' Thomas called to Flood. Then, to Johnson, he said, 'I'm going to give you more of a chance than you ever gave me.'

'You're going to do what?'

'You heard me.'

'The varmints are tied,' Flood sang out.

Thomas nodded, and with eyes going to slits he said, 'I'm going to give you a chance to draw, Johnson.' And he holstered his gun.

The man stood very still. Sweat poured from his brow. He glanced back at his men, who were watching him with laughter in their hard eyes.

'Go ahead,' Thomas urged, 'draw, you bastard!'

Johnson shook his head; his hands flapped the air like broken wings.

Thomas' gun leaped free of the holster. For several moments he pointed it at the man. His finger tightened on the trigger, but he couldn't squeeze it, at least not at a man who was too frightened to defend himself. For several moments he pointed the gun at the man.

Thomas glanced at the men. Their faces were filled with the lust for blood. It didn't matter to them if it was his blood or Johnson's…

He had seen a river of blood. He had helped fill it, and now he was about to add to it again…

Thomas shook his head. He wasn't going to do it. He wasn't going to make it easy for Johnson. And he said, 'You're not worth killing.' He thrust his gun back into the holster. 'Next time,' he said in a flat voice, 'I'll kill you. Now mount up and take your trash with you. Ride!'

Johnson scrambled to his horse, and moments later he and his men were kicking up dust.

'Let's get our herd together,' Thomas told his segundo. 'We've got a drive to finish!'

The last cow made it up the north bank of the Brazos just as the sun was setting. After the herd was bedded down, Thomas rode around it. He was sure now that he would make it all the way to Kansas City in time to be home before the first snow came.

He petted his mount's neck, and thought about playing with his son…

A NOTE TO THE READER

Dear Reader,

If you have enjoyed the novel enough to leave a review on **Amazon** and **Goodreads**, then we would be truly grateful.

Sapere Books

Sapere Books is an exciting new publisher of brilliant fiction and popular history.

To find out more about our latest releases and our monthly bargain books visit our website: **saperebooks.com**

www.ingramcontent.com/pod-product-compliance
Lightning Source LLC
Chambersburg PA
CBHW051803050726
47598CB00006B/2401